AROUND THE WORLD IN 80 PUZZLES

ALEKSANDRA ARTYMOWSKA

First U.S. edition 2018

Library of Congress Catalog Card Number pending
ISBN 978-1-5362-0308-0

18 19 20 21 22 23 TLF 10 9 8 7 6 5 4 3 2 1

Printed in Dongguan, Guangdong, China

This book was typeset in Amatic SC.
The illustrations were done in pen and ink and colored digitally.

BIG PICTURE PRESS
an imprint of
Candlewick Press
99 Dover Street
Somerville, Massachusetts 02144

www.candlewick.com

Around the World in 80 Puzzles

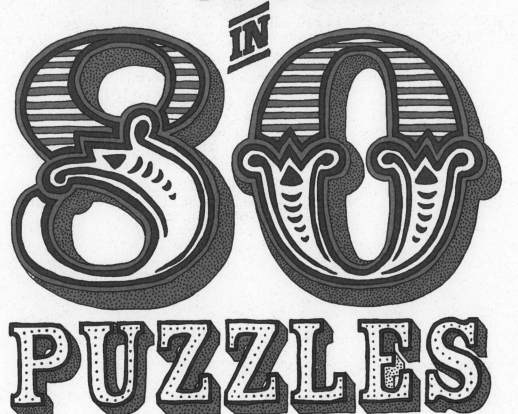

ALEKSANDRA ARTYMOWSKA

BPP

DEAR READER,

DO YOU DREAM OF ADVENTURE? DO YOU
WANT TO BE JUST LIKE THE CHARACTERS IN YOUR
FAVORITE BOOKS? YES? THEN READ ON . . .

THIS LETTER IS ONLY THE BEGINNING OF
YOUR JOURNEY — AN EXPEDITION THAT WILL
TAKE YOU AROUND THE WORLD IN 80 PUZZLES.
CAN YOU COMPLETE THEM ALL?

JUST GRAB ON TO THE BALLOON TO SET SAIL.

BON VOYAGE!

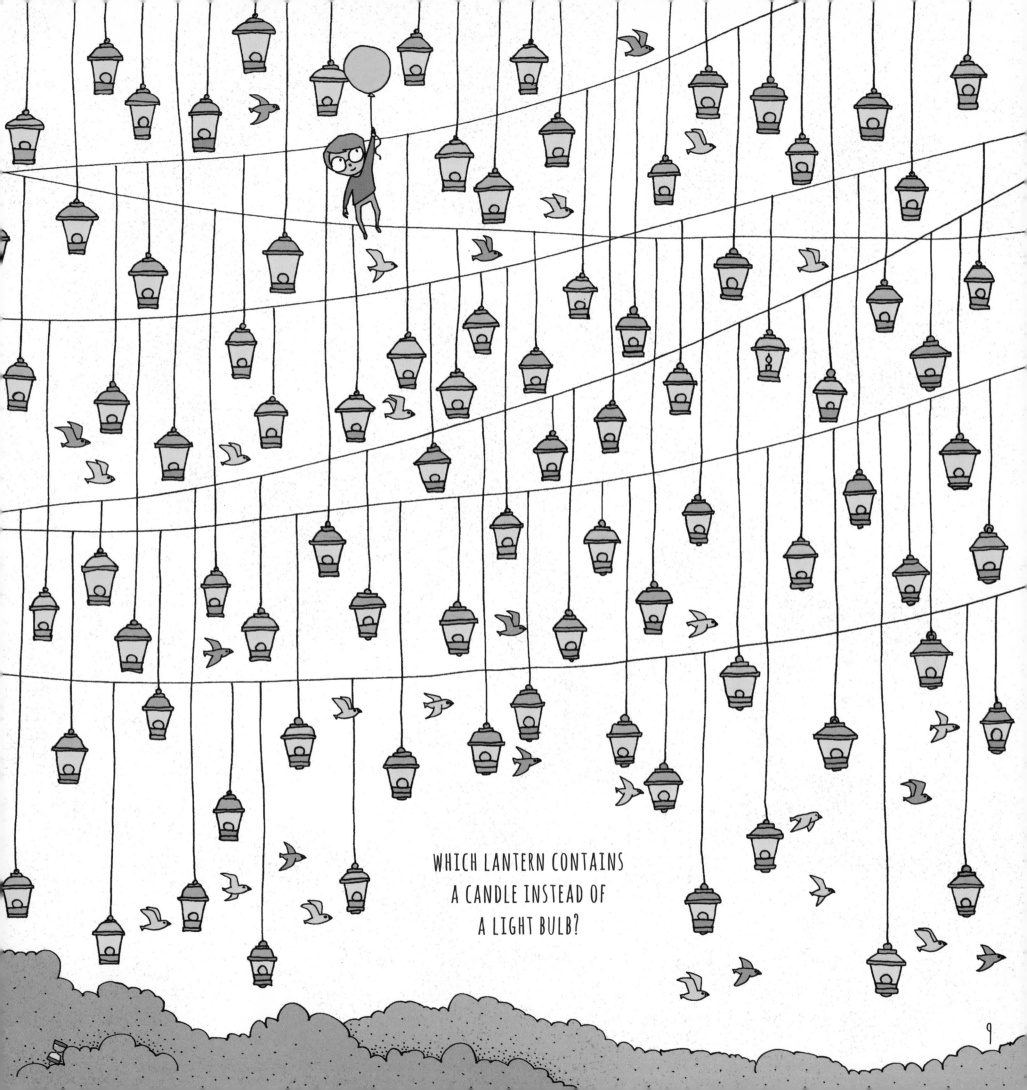

WHICH LANTERN CONTAINS
A CANDLE INSTEAD OF
A LIGHT BULB?

ALL OF THE HOT-AIR
BALLOONS EXCEPT ONE ARE
CARRYING AN ARMCHAIR.
CAN YOU FIND THE
ODD ONE OUT?

CAN YOU SPOT
3 BALLOONS WITH
IDENTICAL PATTERNS?

11

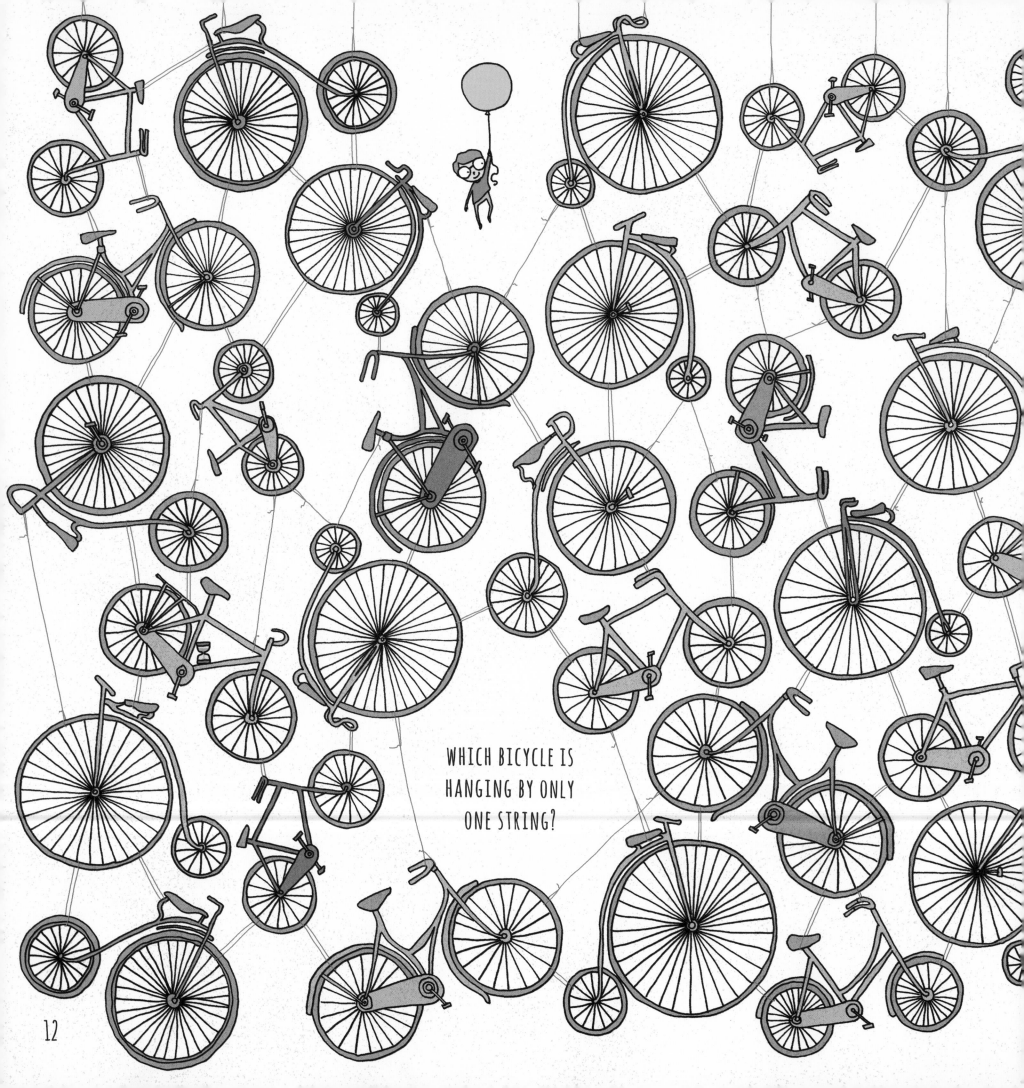

WHICH BICYCLE IS
HANGING BY ONLY
ONE STRING?

12

FIND A HIDDEN PAIR
OF SCISSORS TO CUT
THE BICYCLE FREE!

13

WHICH OF THESE PIECES IS NOT PART OF THE EIFFEL TOWER?

CAN YOU ARRANGE THE
OTHER PIECES IN
THE CORRECT ORDER?

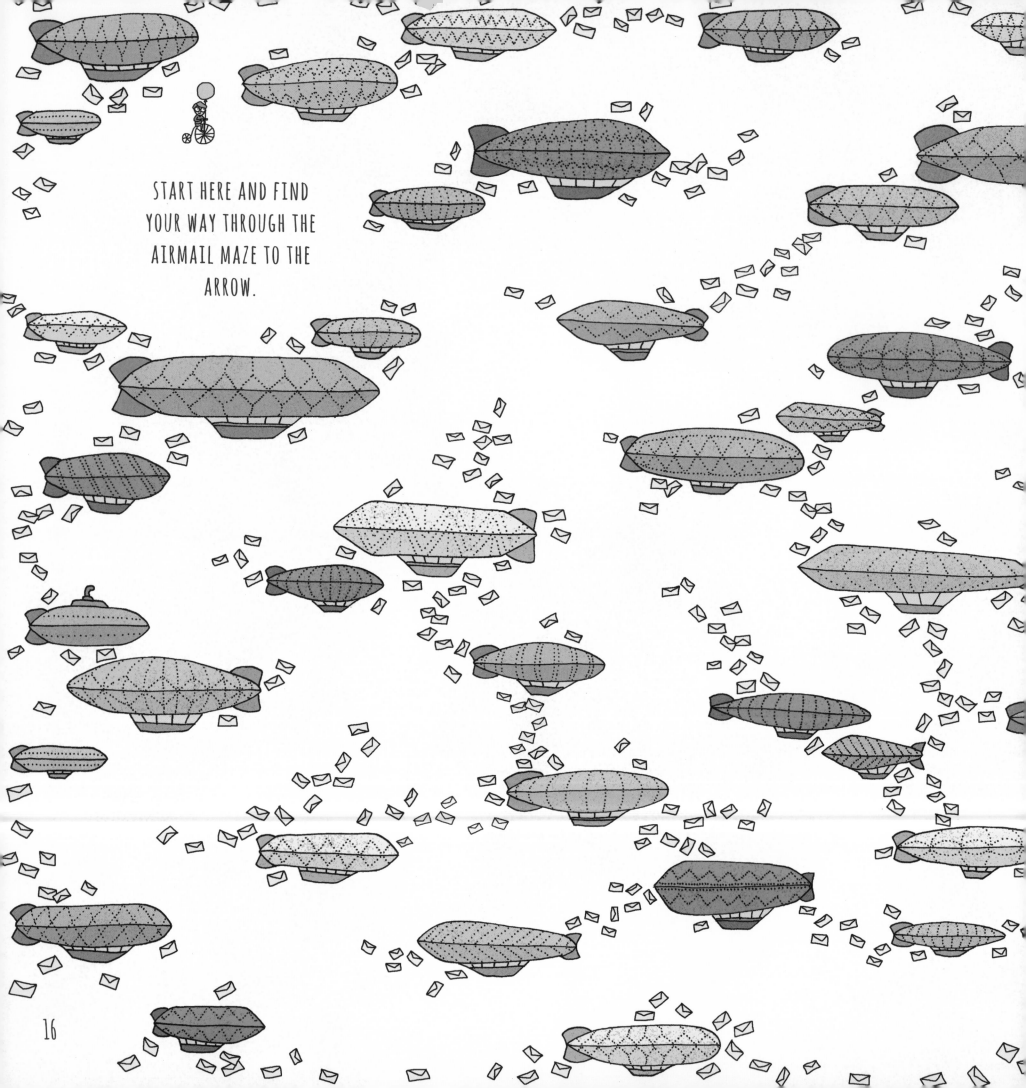

START HERE AND FIND YOUR WAY THROUGH THE AIRMAIL MAZE TO THE ARROW.

16

CAN YOU SEE ONE
SUBMARINE HIDING AMONG
THE AIRSHIPS?

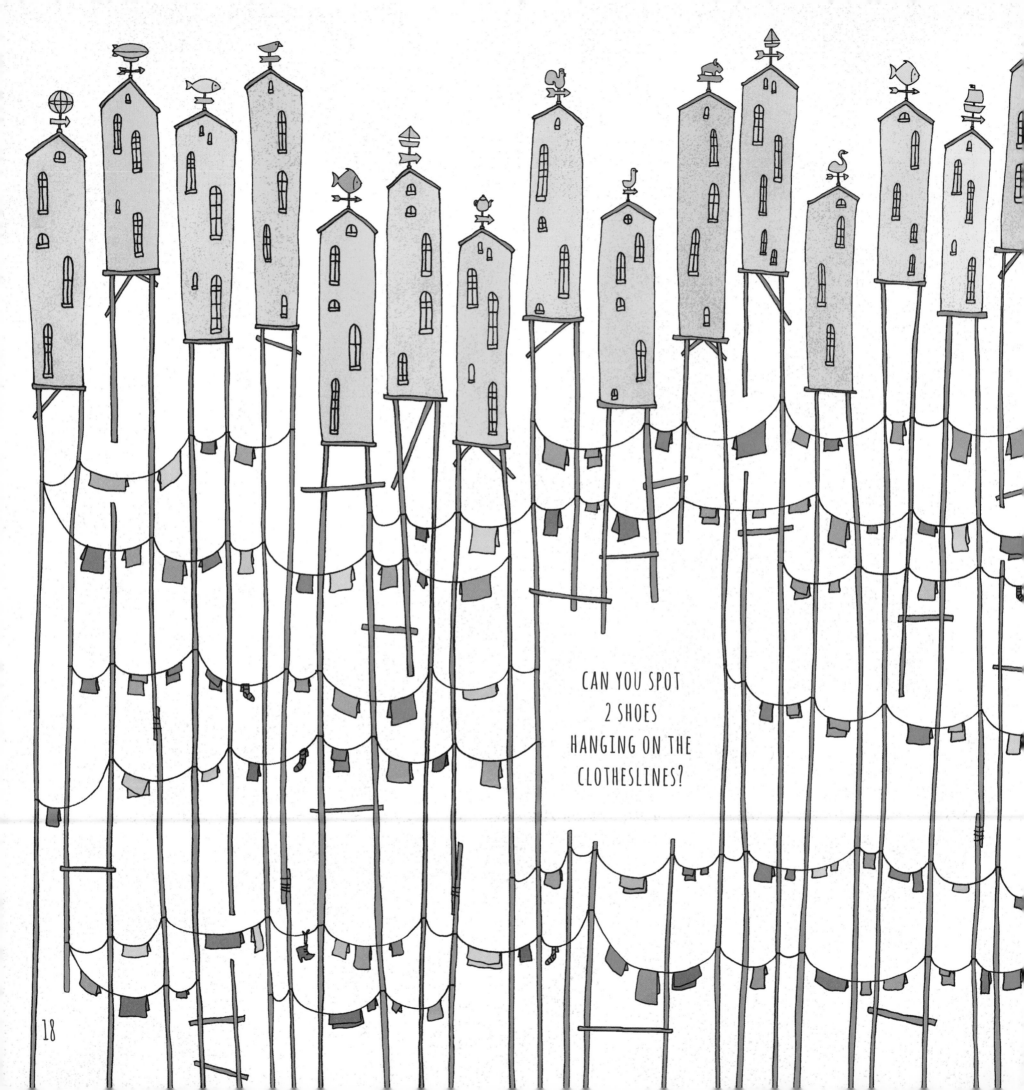

CAN YOU SPOT
2 SHOES
HANGING ON THE
CLOTHESLINES?

18

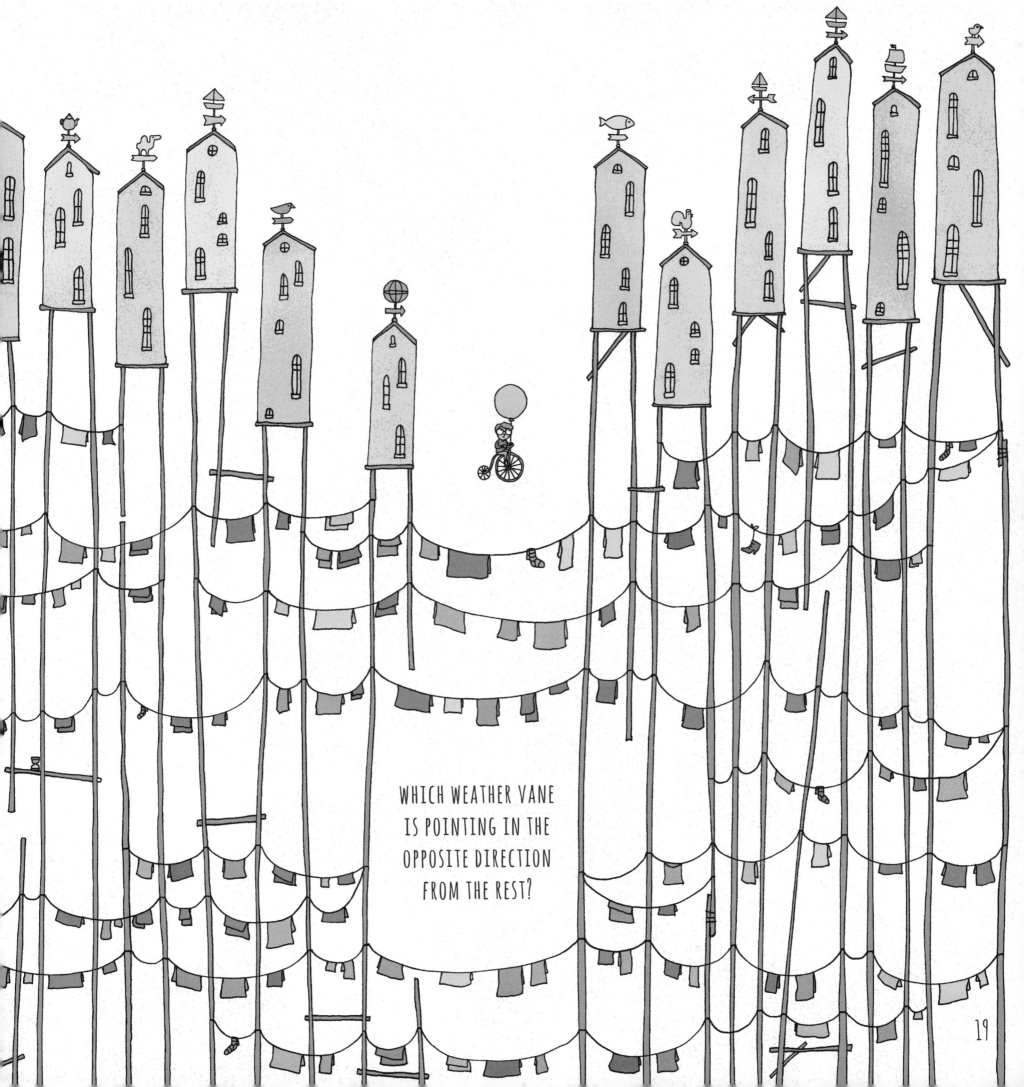

WHICH WEATHER VANE
IS POINTING IN THE
OPPOSITE DIRECTION
FROM THE REST?

19

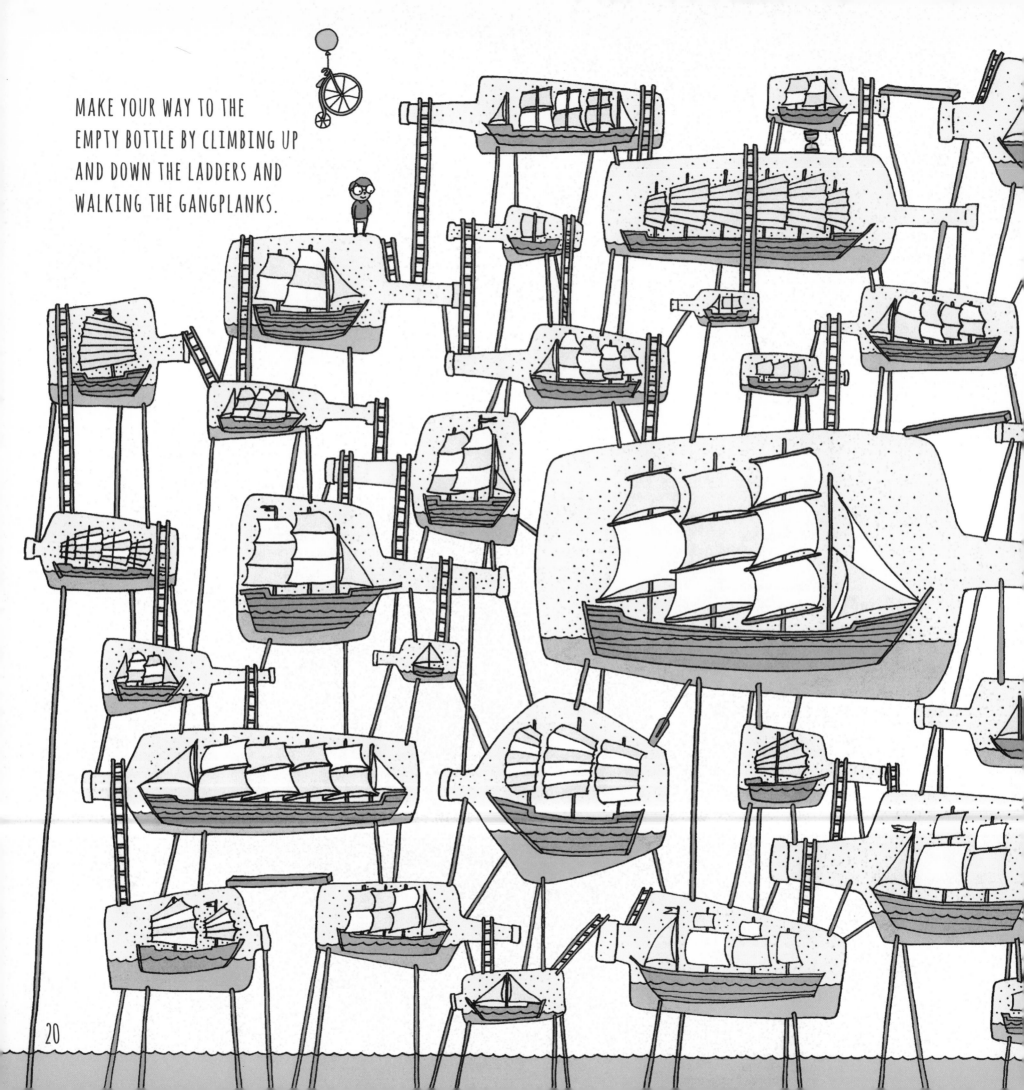

MAKE YOUR WAY TO THE
EMPTY BOTTLE BY CLIMBING UP
AND DOWN THE LADDERS AND
WALKING THE GANGPLANKS.

THERE'S A PADDLE HIDDEN
SOMEWHERE IN THE SCENE.
CAN YOU FIND IT?

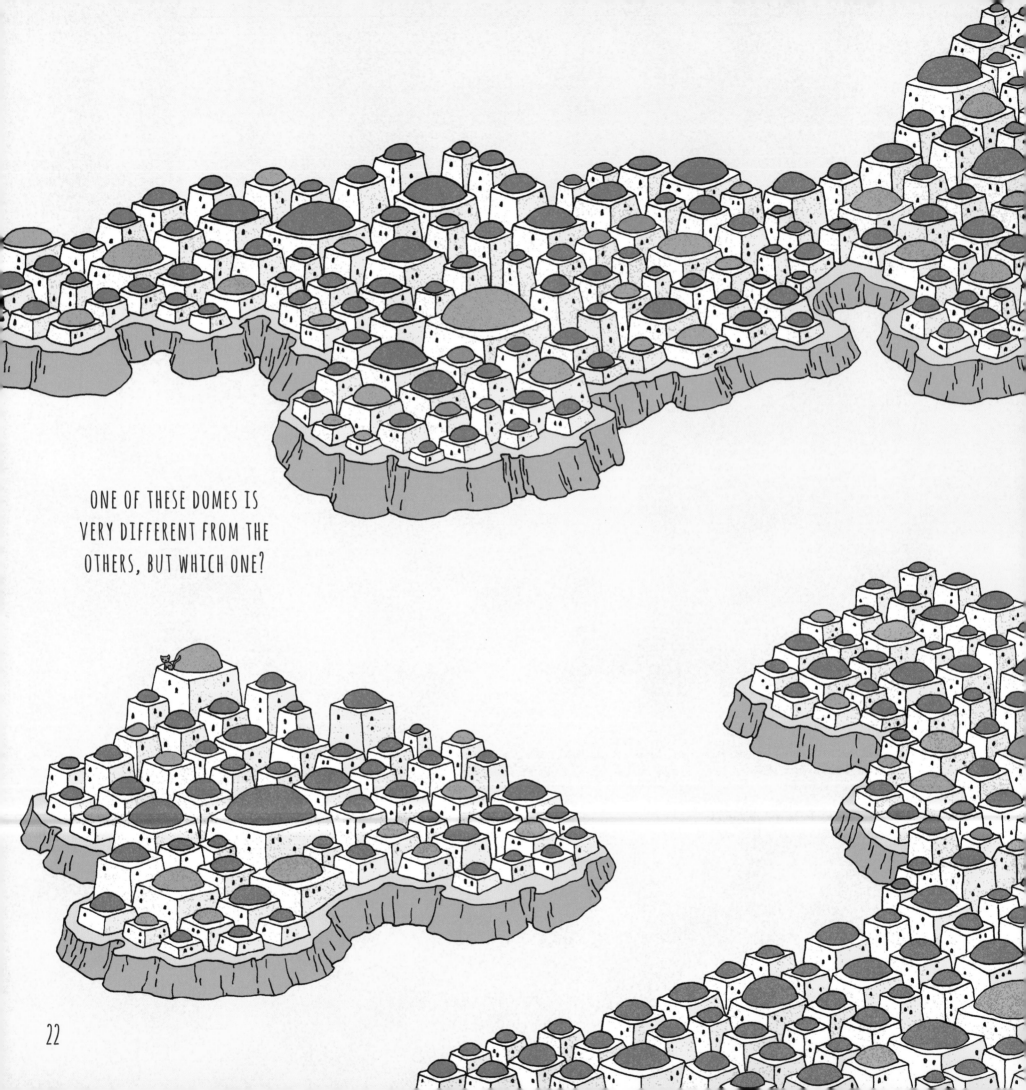

ONE OF THESE DOMES IS
VERY DIFFERENT FROM THE
OTHERS, BUT WHICH ONE?

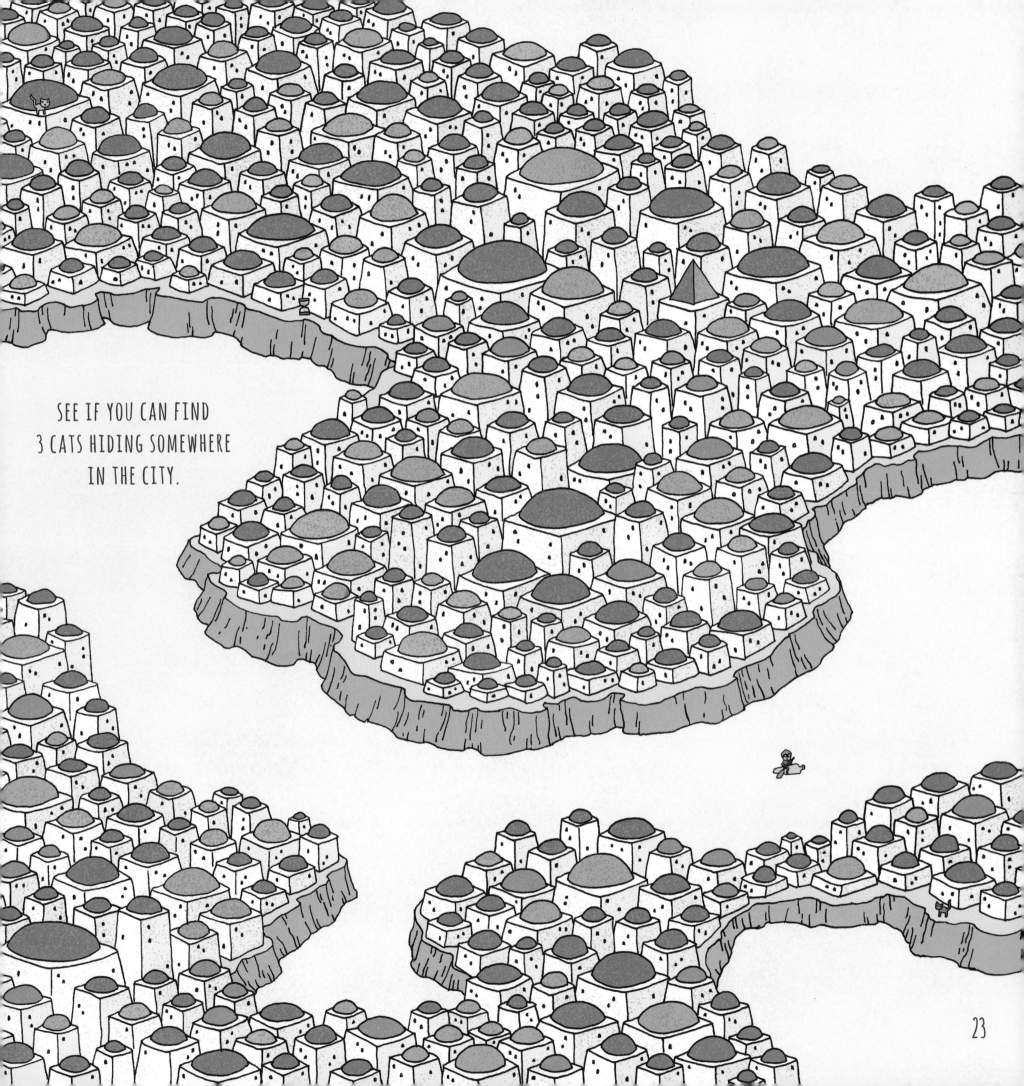

SEE IF YOU CAN FIND
3 CATS HIDING SOMEWHERE
IN THE CITY.

23

CAN YOU SEE ONE
ARCHWAY WITH NO GREEN
TILES AROUND IT?

24

NOW LOOK FOR
3 LIZARDS HIDING
AGAINST THE WALL.

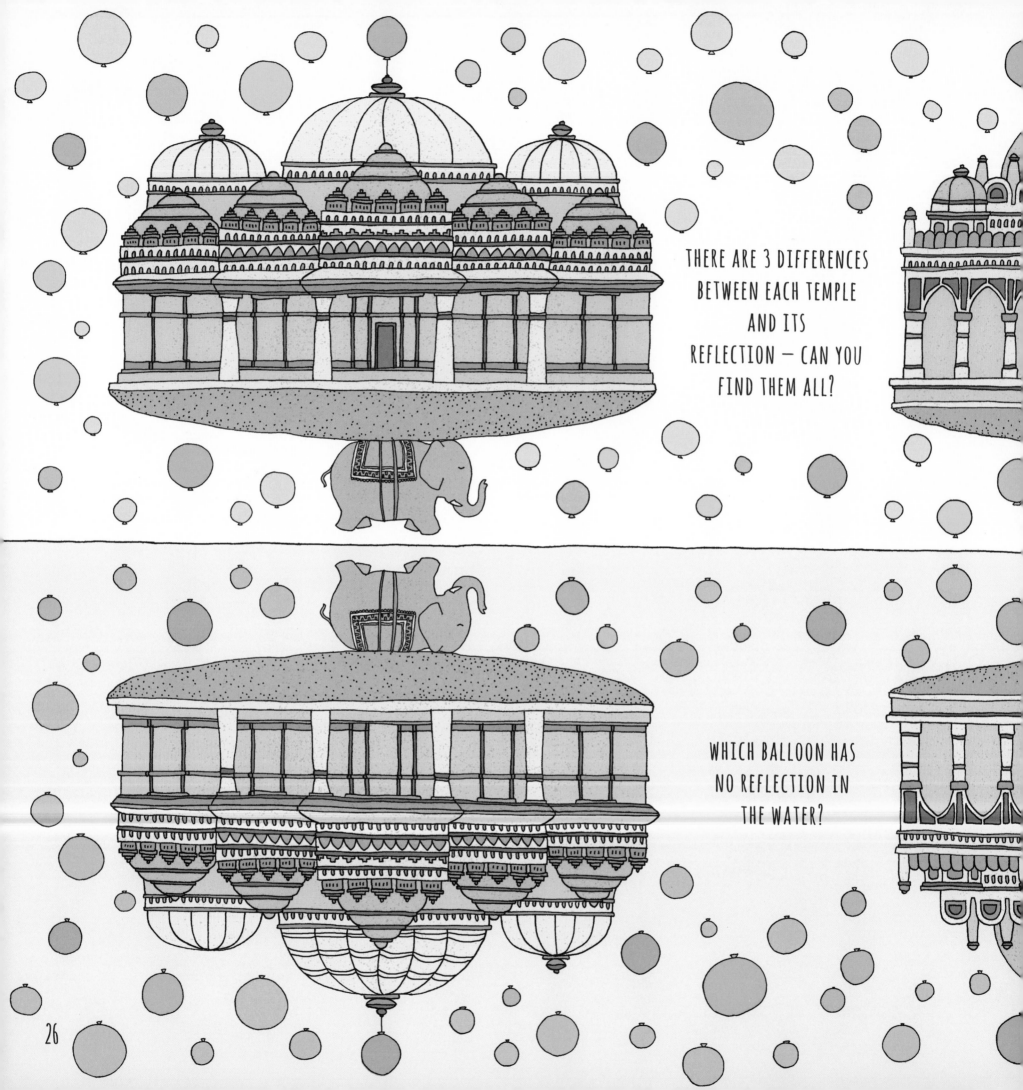

THERE ARE 3 DIFFERENCES BETWEEN EACH TEMPLE AND ITS REFLECTION — CAN YOU FIND THEM ALL?

WHICH BALLOON HAS NO REFLECTION IN THE WATER?

26

MAKE YOUR WAY THROUGH THE MAZE TO A FELLOW TRAVELER, THEN GO DOWN TO THE SMALLEST BOAT.

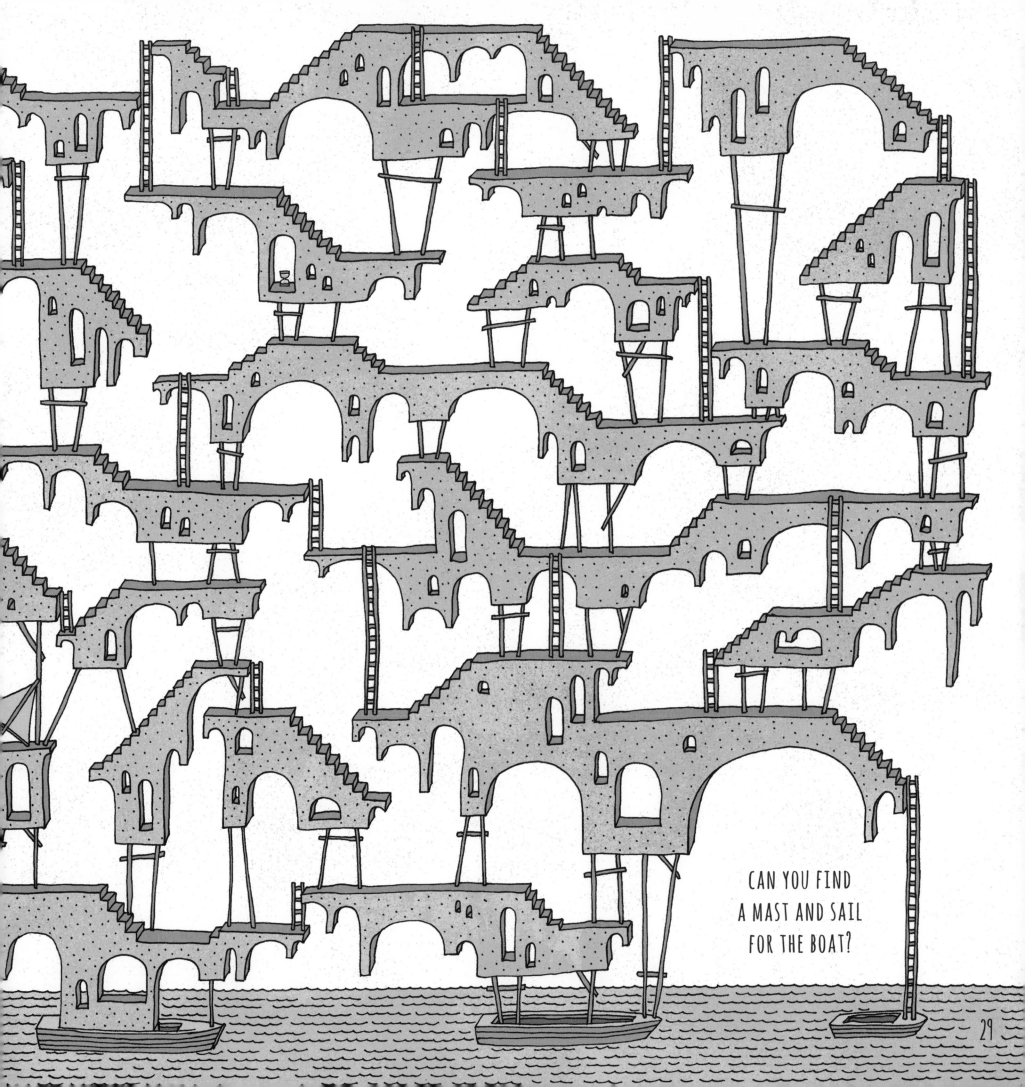

CAN YOU FIND
A MAST AND SAIL
FOR THE BOAT?

THERE'S A SNAKE HIDING
IN THE JUNGLE VINES.
CAN YOU SEE IT?

30

HOW MANY NOISY PARROTS
CAN YOU SPOT?

31

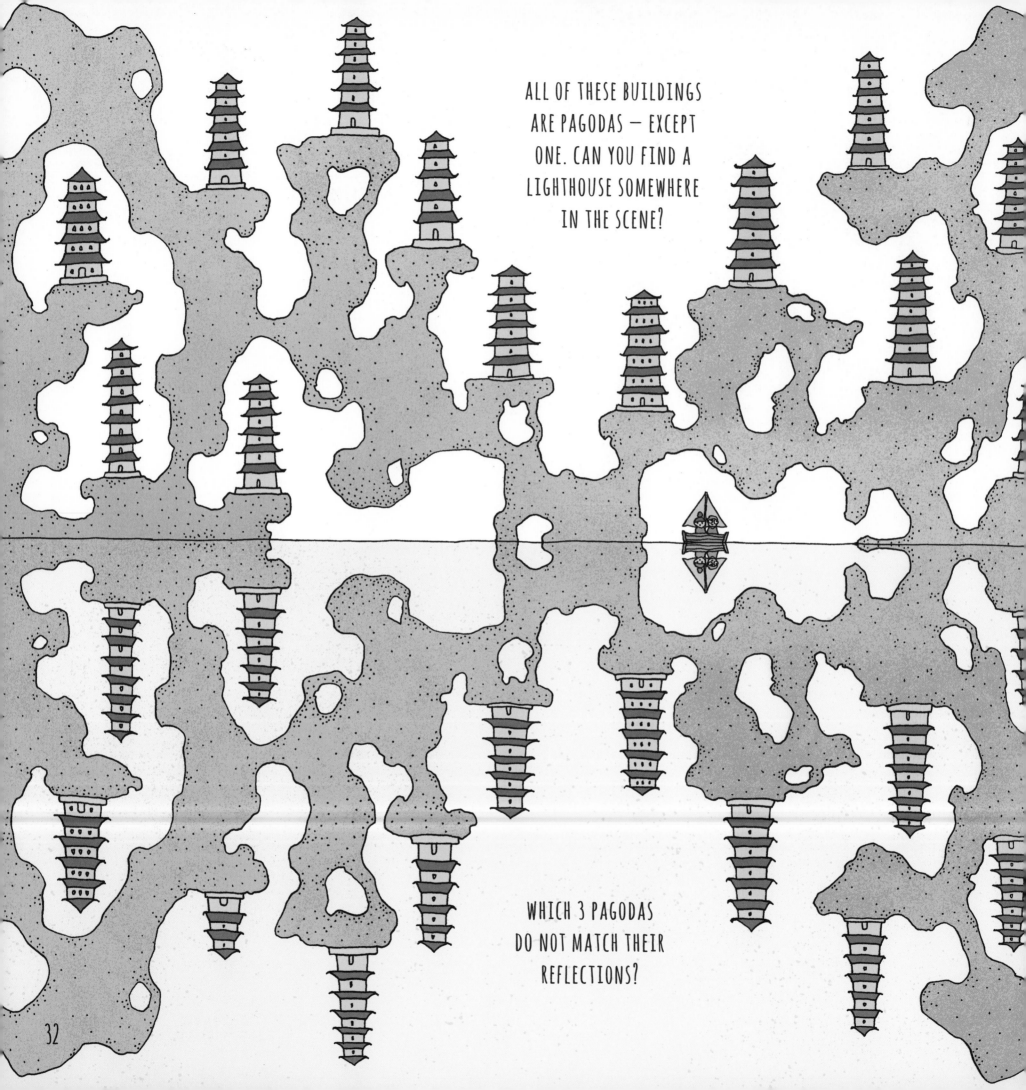

ALL OF THESE BUILDINGS
ARE PAGODAS — EXCEPT
ONE. CAN YOU FIND A
LIGHTHOUSE SOMEWHERE
IN THE SCENE?

WHICH 3 PAGODAS
DO NOT MATCH THEIR
REFLECTIONS?

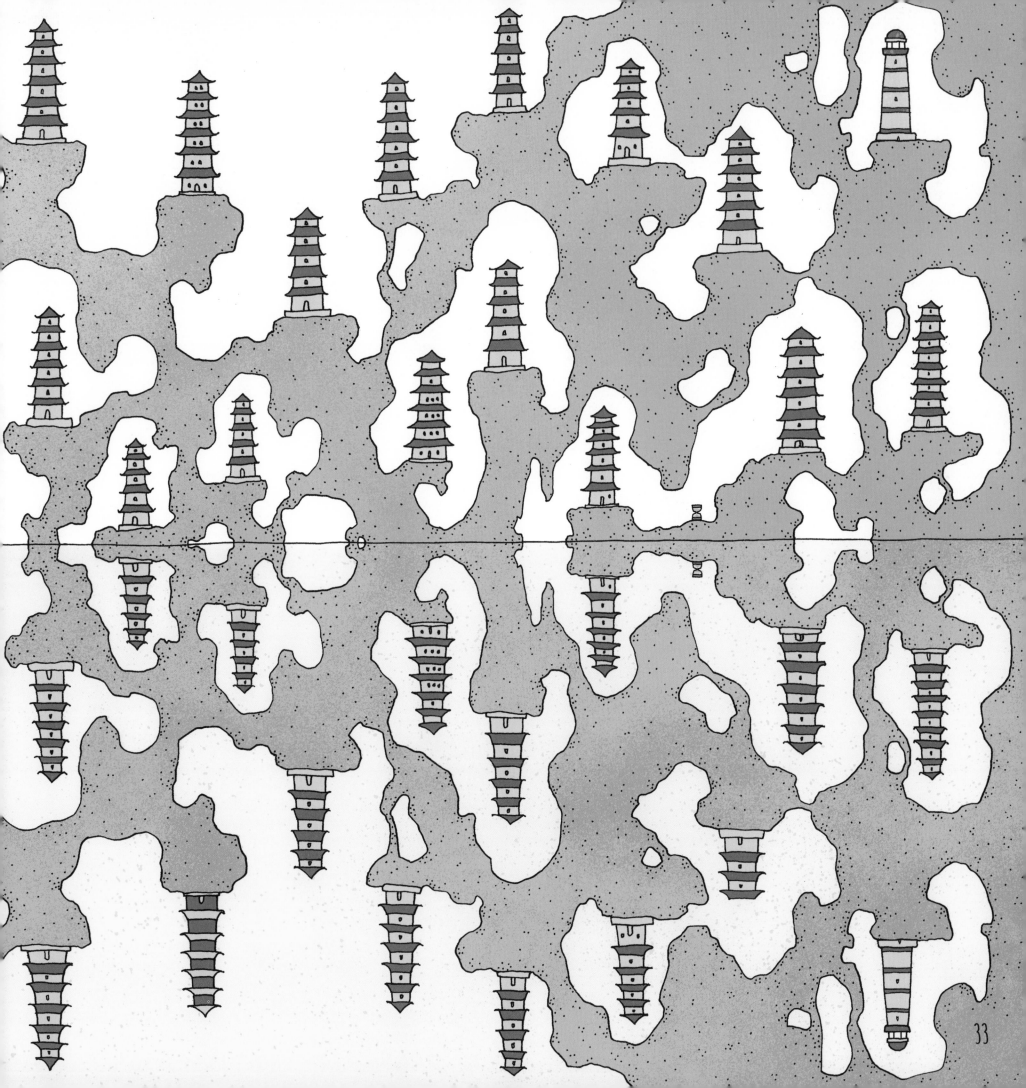

THERE ARE 2 BEETLES HIDING IN THE COLORFUL TILES. DO YOU SEE THEM?

34

CAN YOU MATCH THE FALLEN PIECES TO THE ARCHES THEY COME FROM?

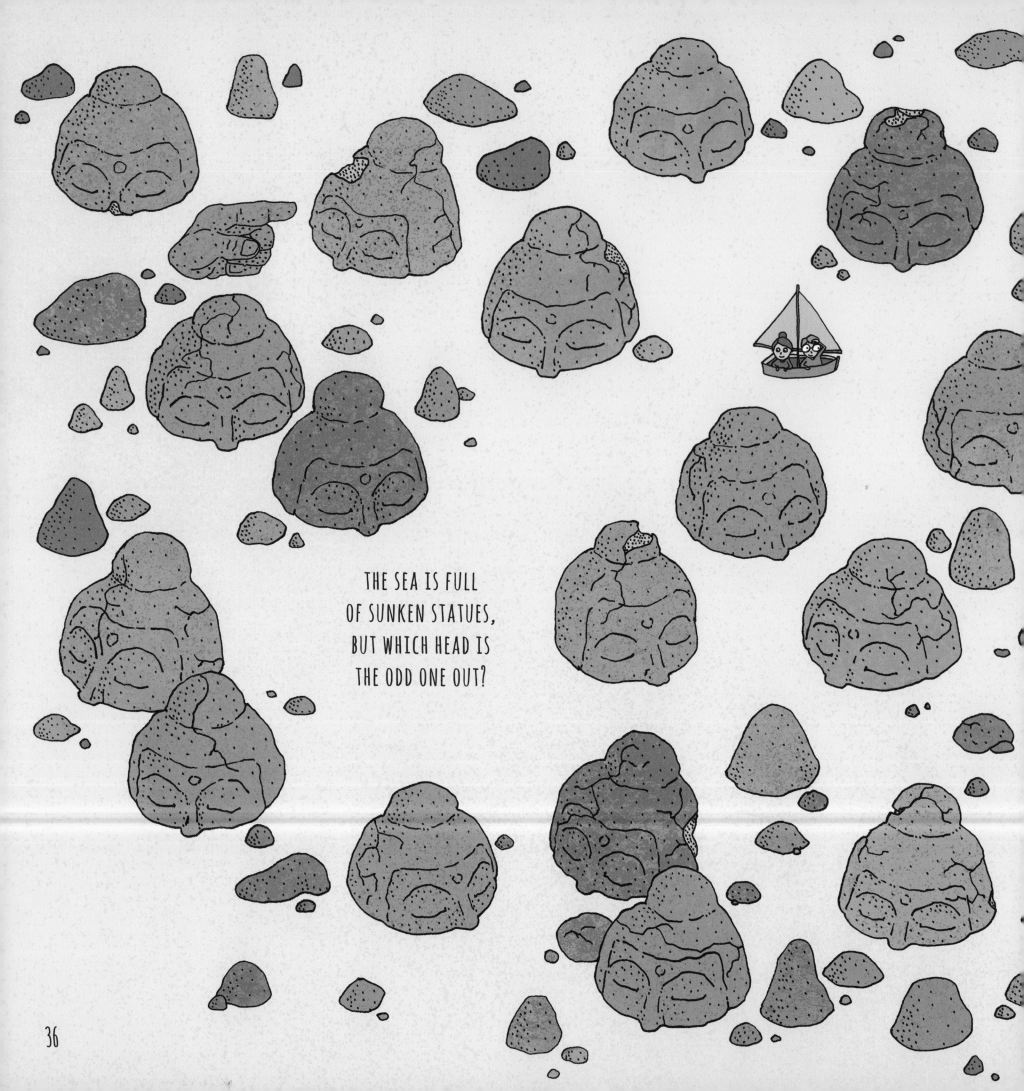

THE SEA IS FULL
OF SUNKEN STATUES,
BUT WHICH HEAD IS
THE ODD ONE OUT?

CAN YOU SEE ANY OTHER
PARTS OF THE STATUES
AMONG THE ROCKS?

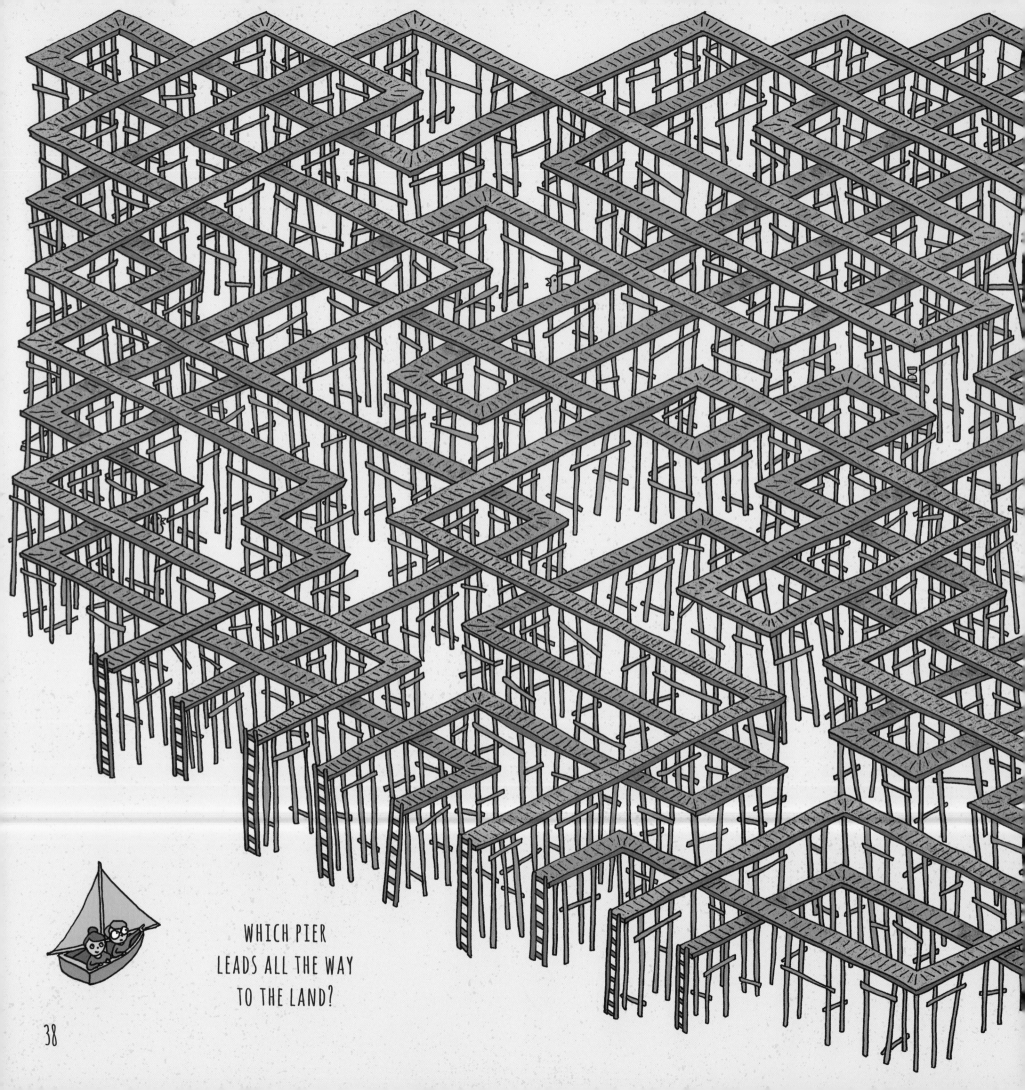

WHICH PIER
LEADS ALL THE WAY
TO THE LAND?

38

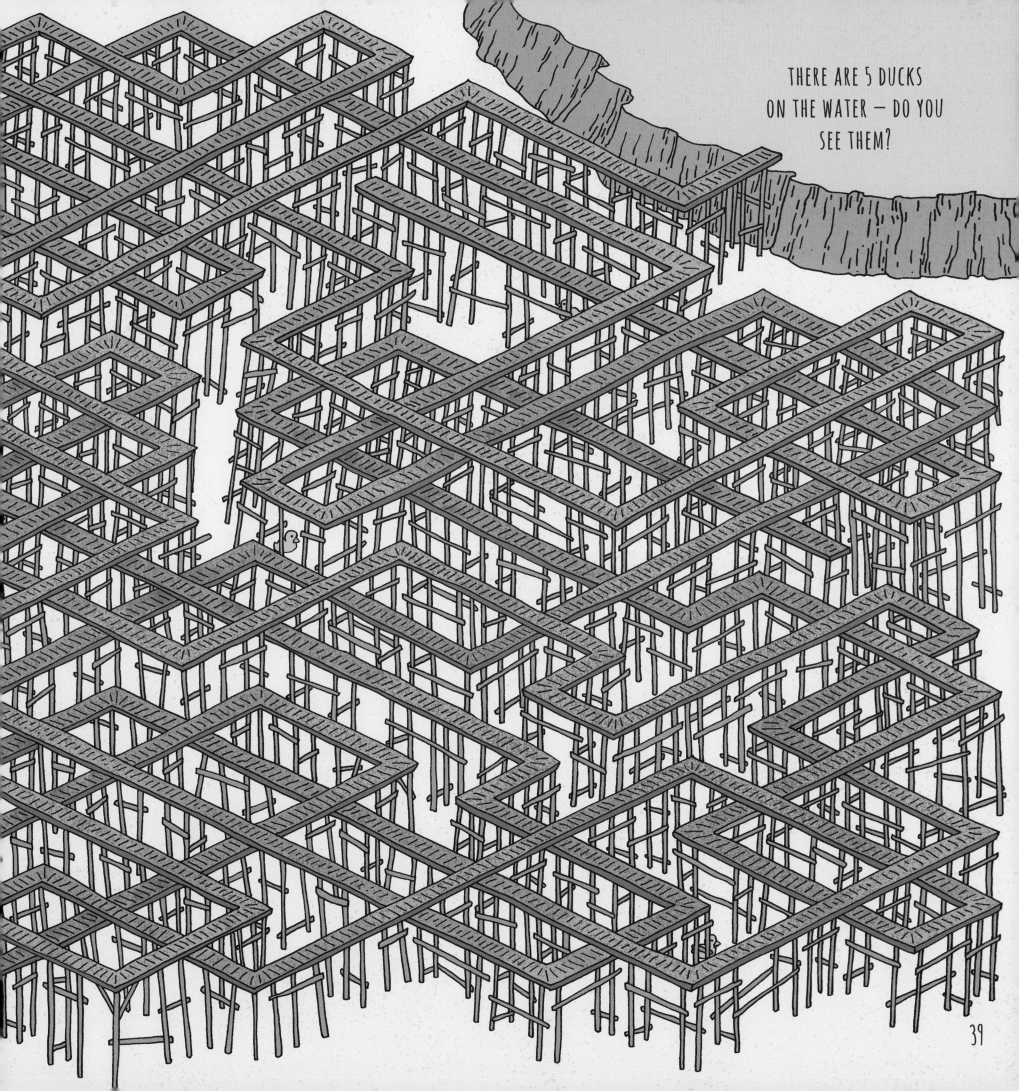

THERE ARE 5 DUCKS ON THE WATER — DO YOU SEE THEM?

39

FIND A SAFE PATH TO THE ARROW, AVOIDING ALL THE SCORPIONS.

40

CAN YOU SEE A HAIRY
TARANTULA HIDING
IN THE SCENE?

41

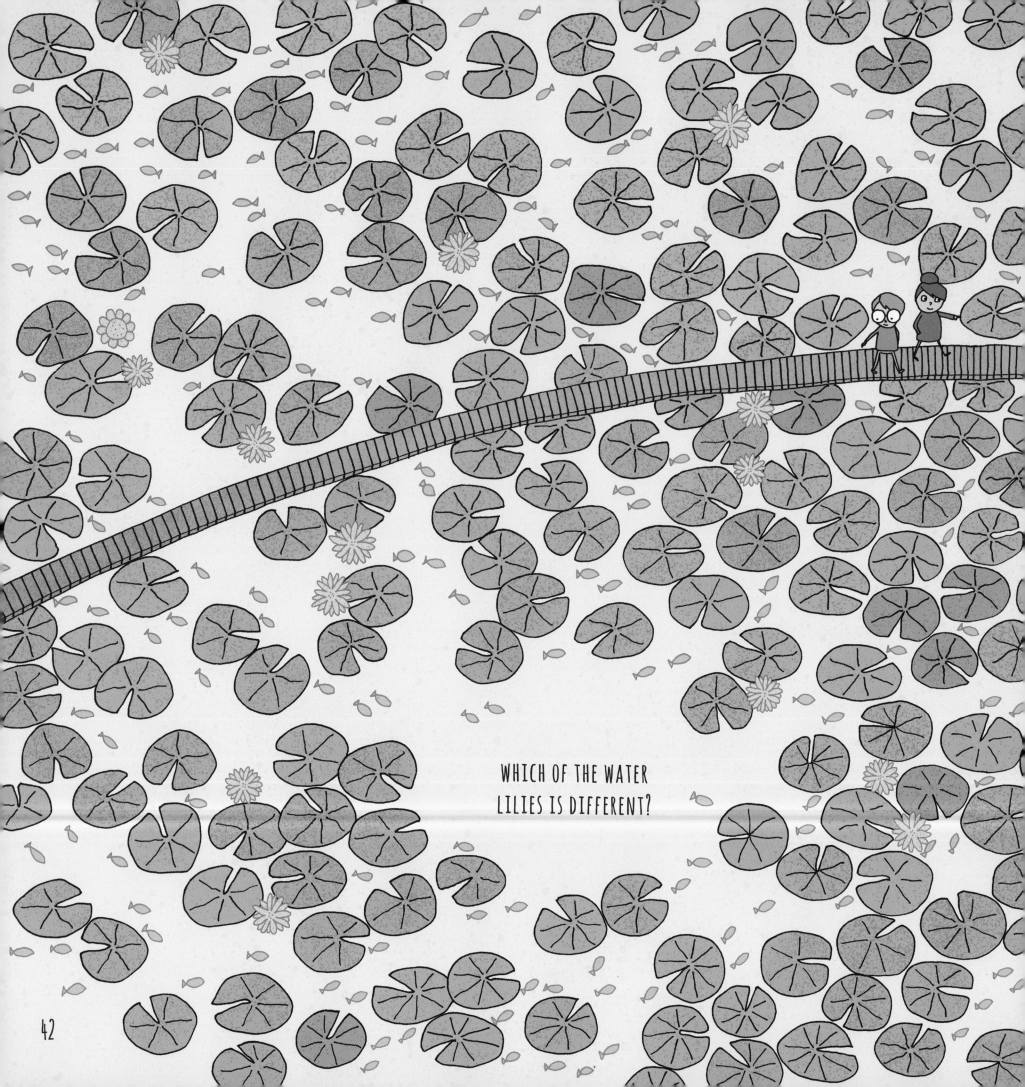

WHICH OF THE WATER
LILIES IS DIFFERENT?

42

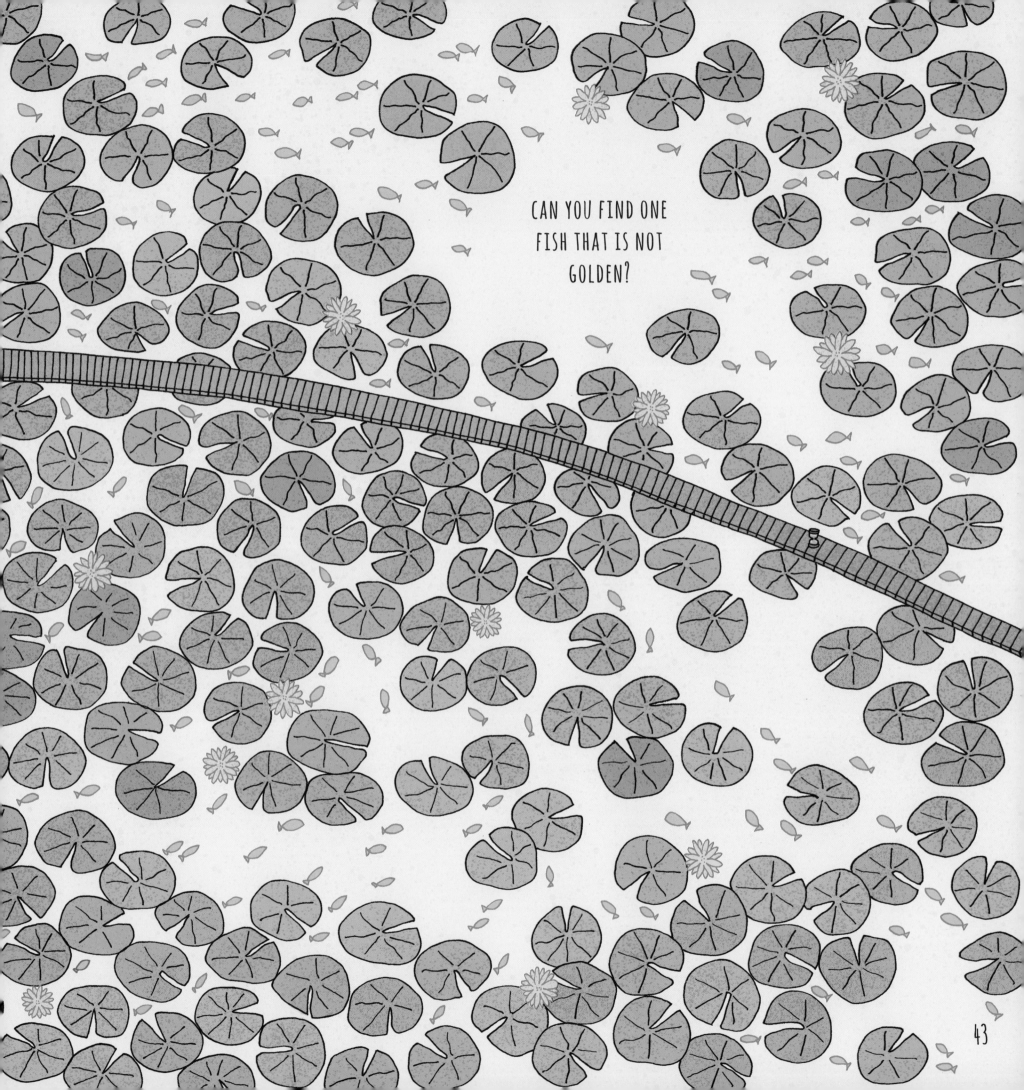

CAN YOU FIND ONE
FISH THAT IS NOT
GOLDEN?

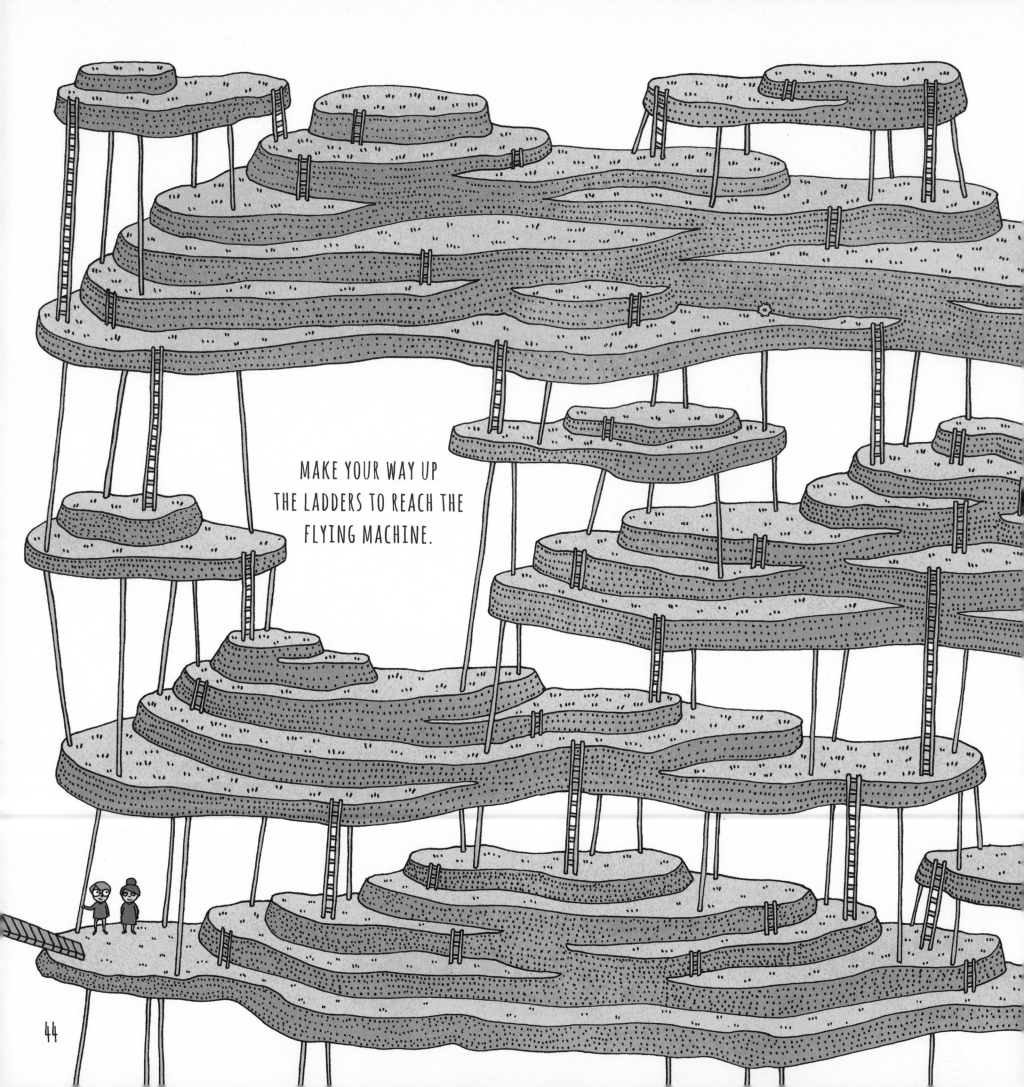

MAKE YOUR WAY UP
THE LADDERS TO REACH THE
FLYING MACHINE.

SEE IF YOU CAN SPOT
2 COGWHEELS SOMEWHERE
IN THE SCENE.

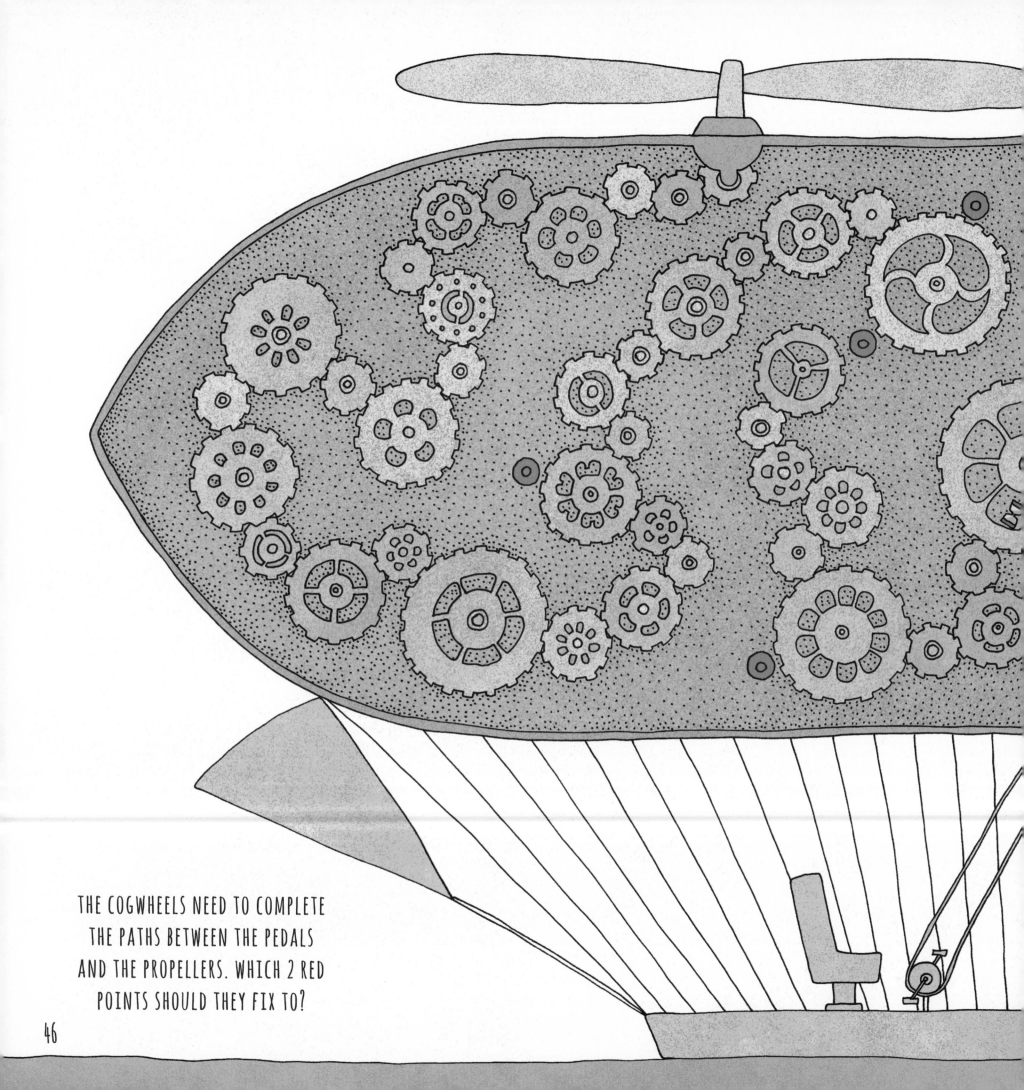

THE COGWHEELS NEED TO COMPLETE
THE PATHS BETWEEN THE PEDALS
AND THE PROPELLERS. WHICH 2 RED
POINTS SHOULD THEY FIX TO?

CAN YOU SPOT A WRENCH LEFT SOMEWHERE INSIDE THE MACHINE?

THERE ARE 5 DIFFERENCES BETWEEN THE TEMPLES. CAN YOU SPOT THEM ALL?

FOLLOW THE LINES TO SEE
WHICH TEMPLE HAS THE
MOST KITES ATTACHED
TO IT.

49

CAN YOU FIND 2 TEAPOTS HANGING AMONG THE LANTERNS?

LOOK FOR A FAN
HIDDEN SOMEWHERE
IN THE SCENE.

WHICH DRAGON HEAD BELONGS WITH WHICH TAIL? TRACE THEIR BODIES THROUGH THE CLOUDS.

CAN YOU FIND 5 BELLS
HANGING INSIDE THE
DRAGONS' BODIES?

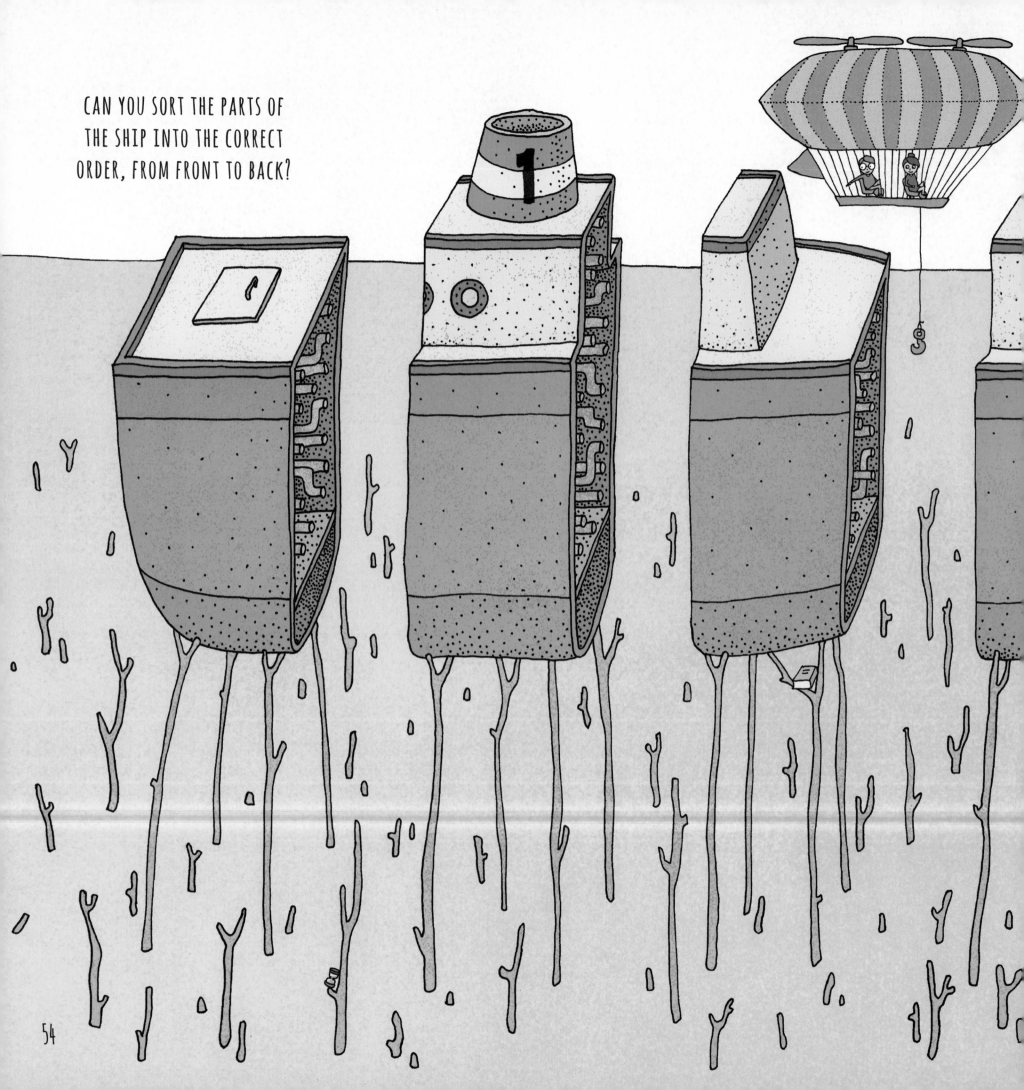

CAN YOU SORT THE PARTS OF THE SHIP INTO THE CORRECT ORDER, FROM FRONT TO BACK?

54

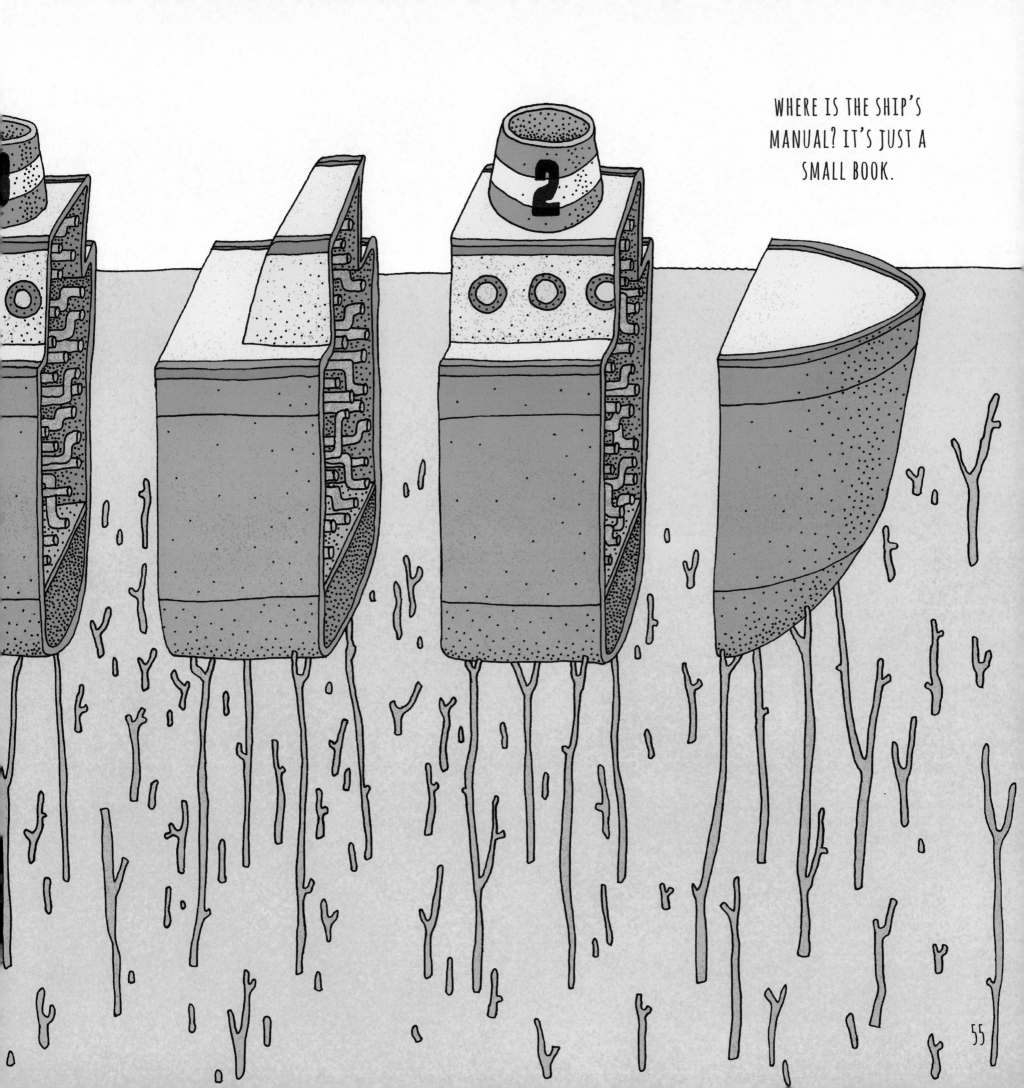

WHERE IS THE SHIP'S MANUAL? IT'S JUST A SMALL BOOK.

55

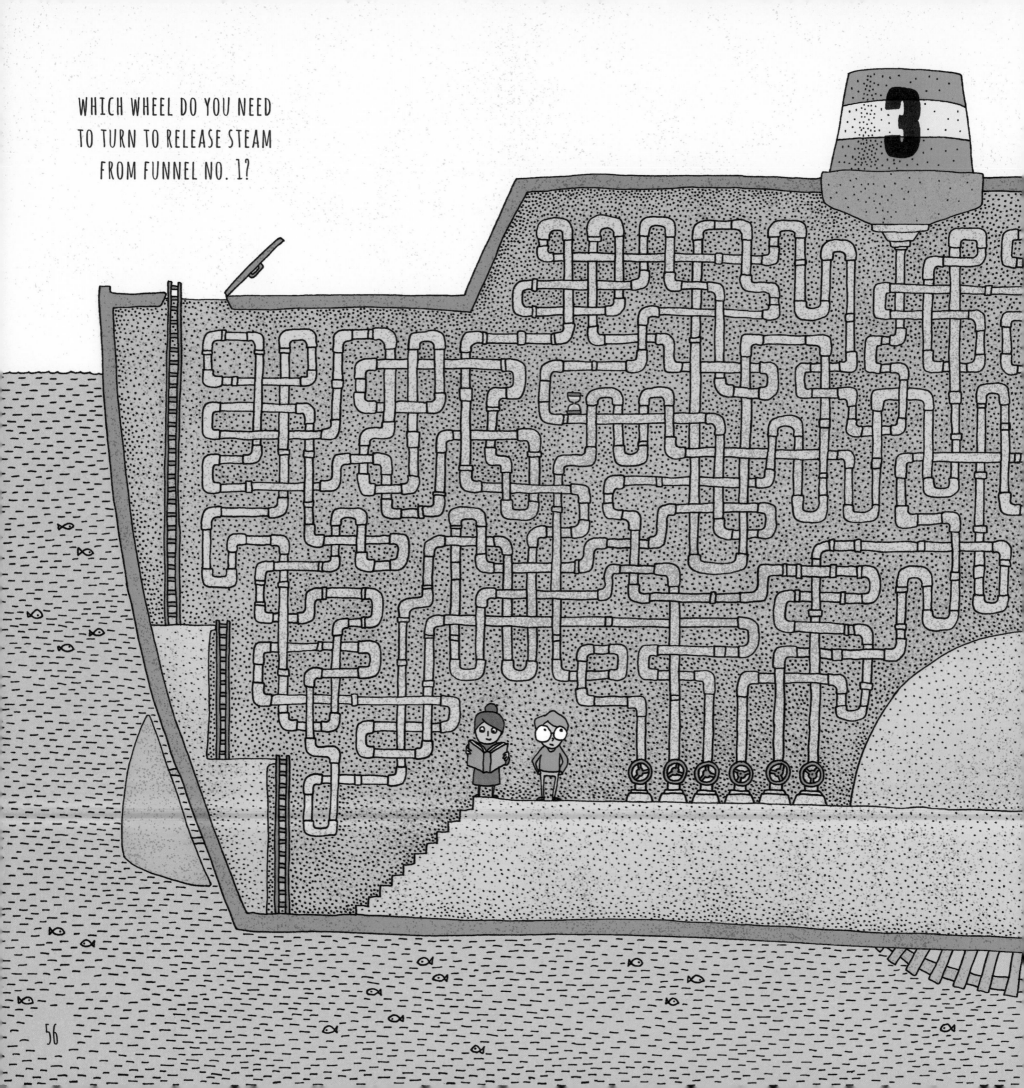

WHICH WHEEL DO YOU NEED TO TURN TO RELEASE STEAM FROM FUNNEL NO. 1?

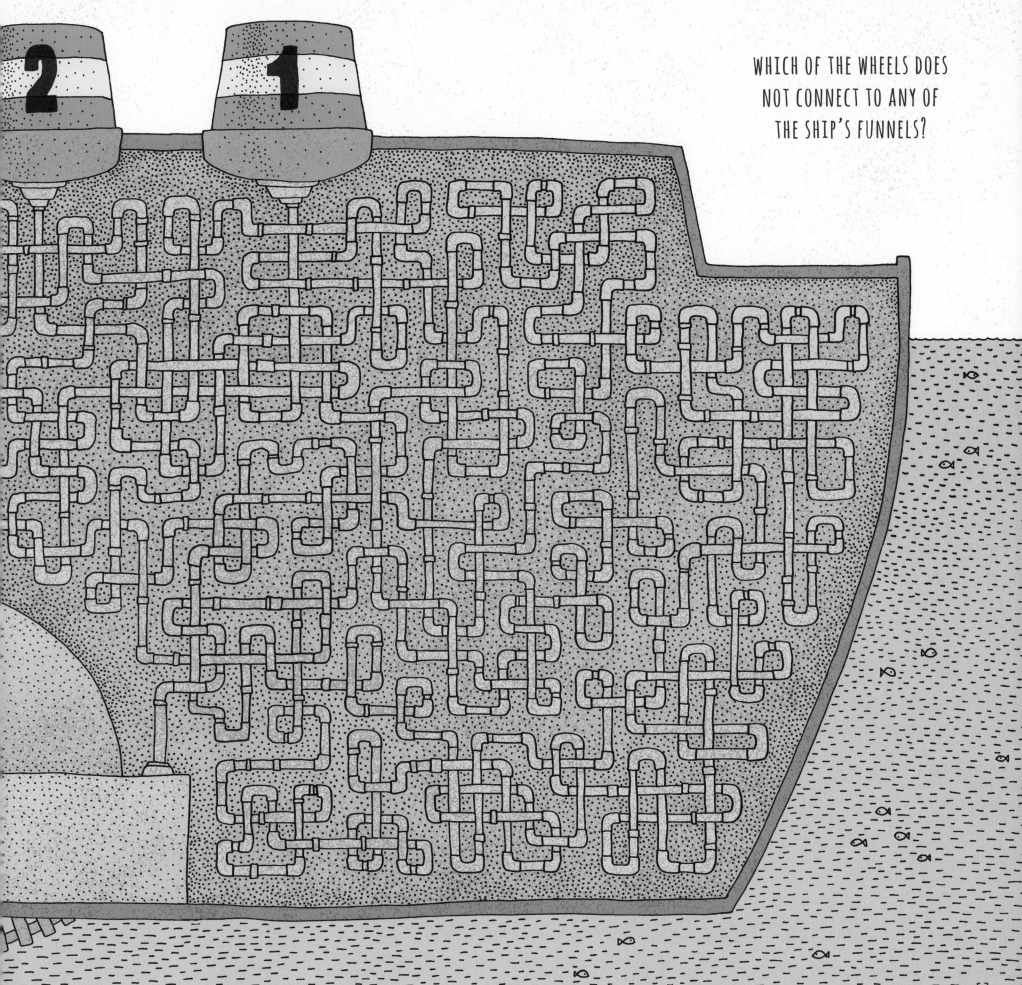

WHICH OF THE WHEELS DOES
NOT CONNECT TO ANY OF
THE SHIP'S FUNNELS?

WHICH OF THESE IS
A CLOUD AND NOT STEAM
FROM A SHIP?

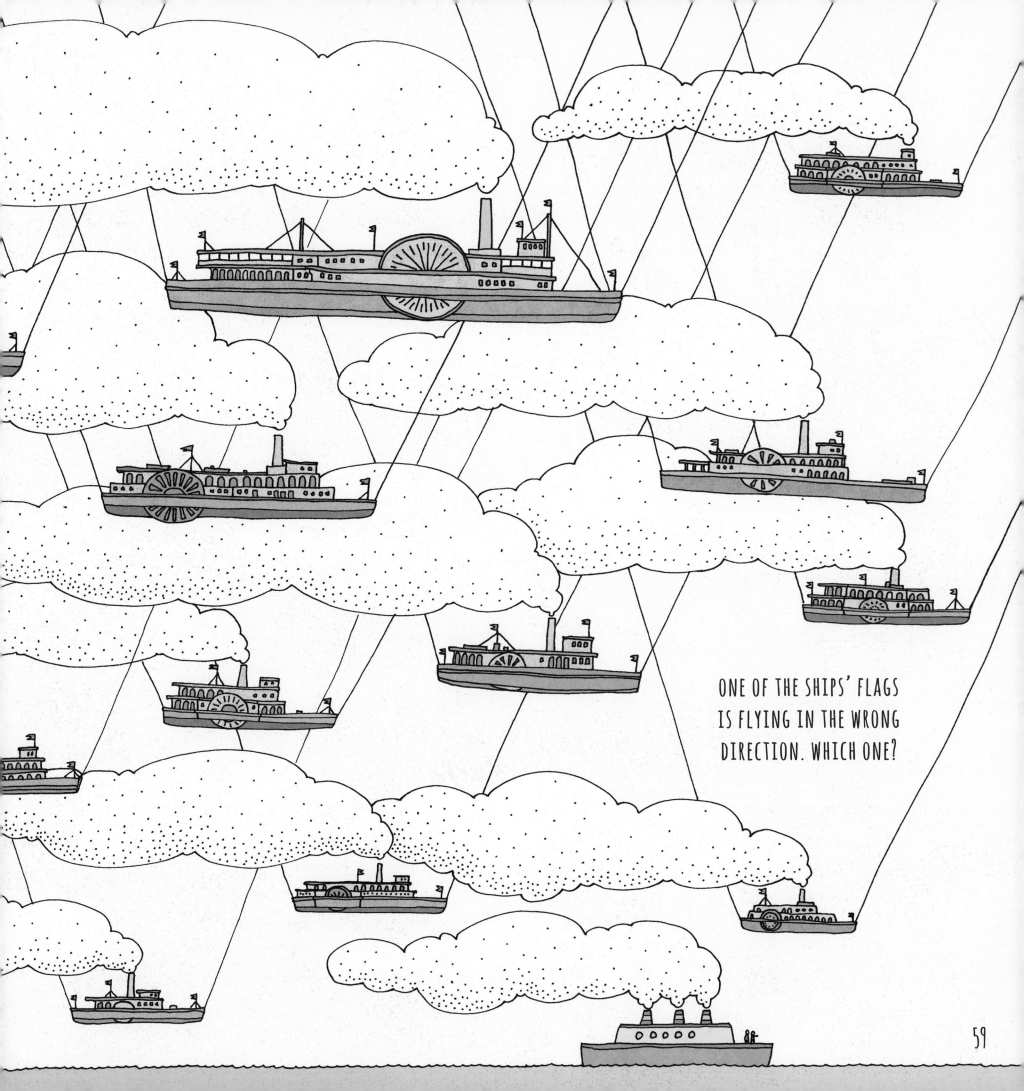

ONE OF THE SHIPS' FLAGS
IS FLYING IN THE WRONG
DIRECTION. WHICH ONE?

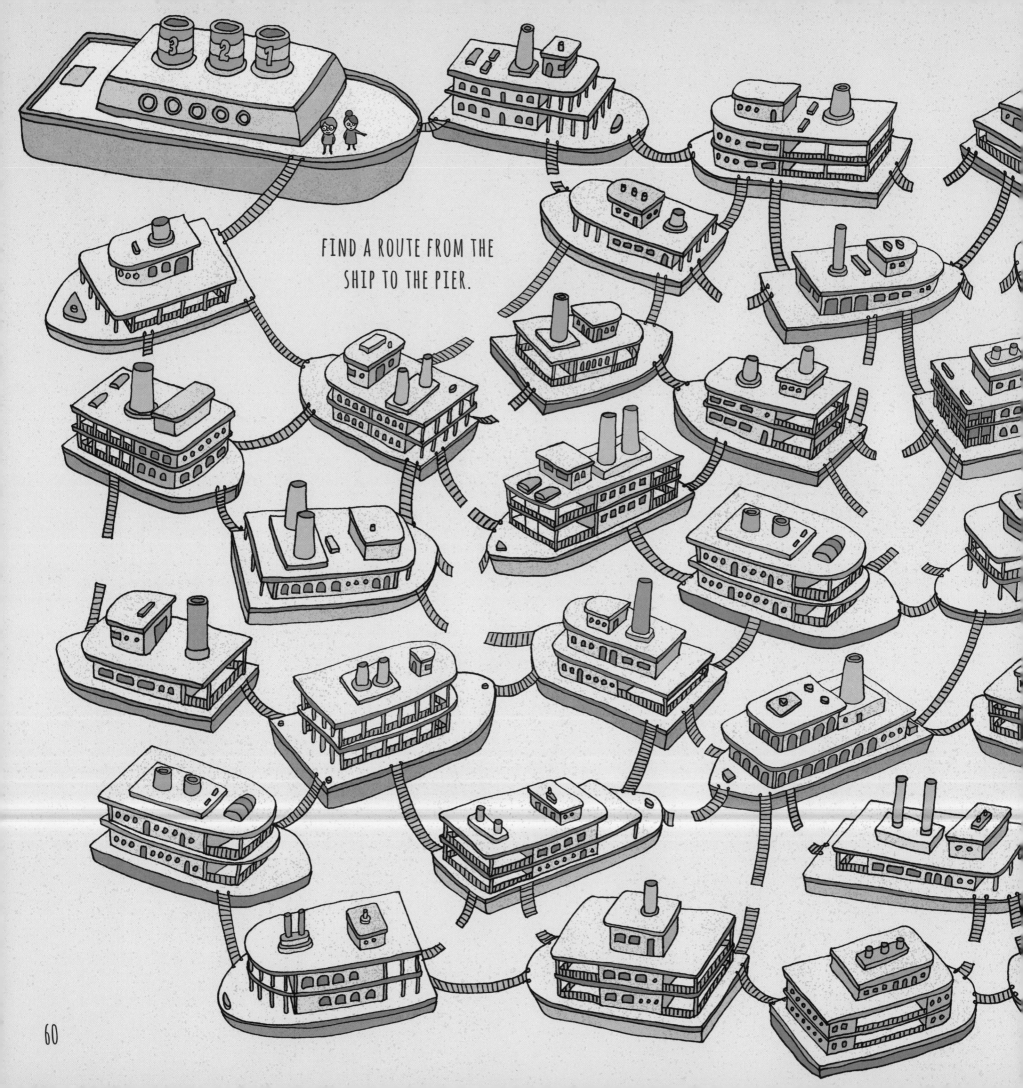

FIND A ROUTE FROM THE
SHIP TO THE PIER.

CAN YOU SPOT
2 IDENTICAL SHIPS
IN THE HARBOR?

61

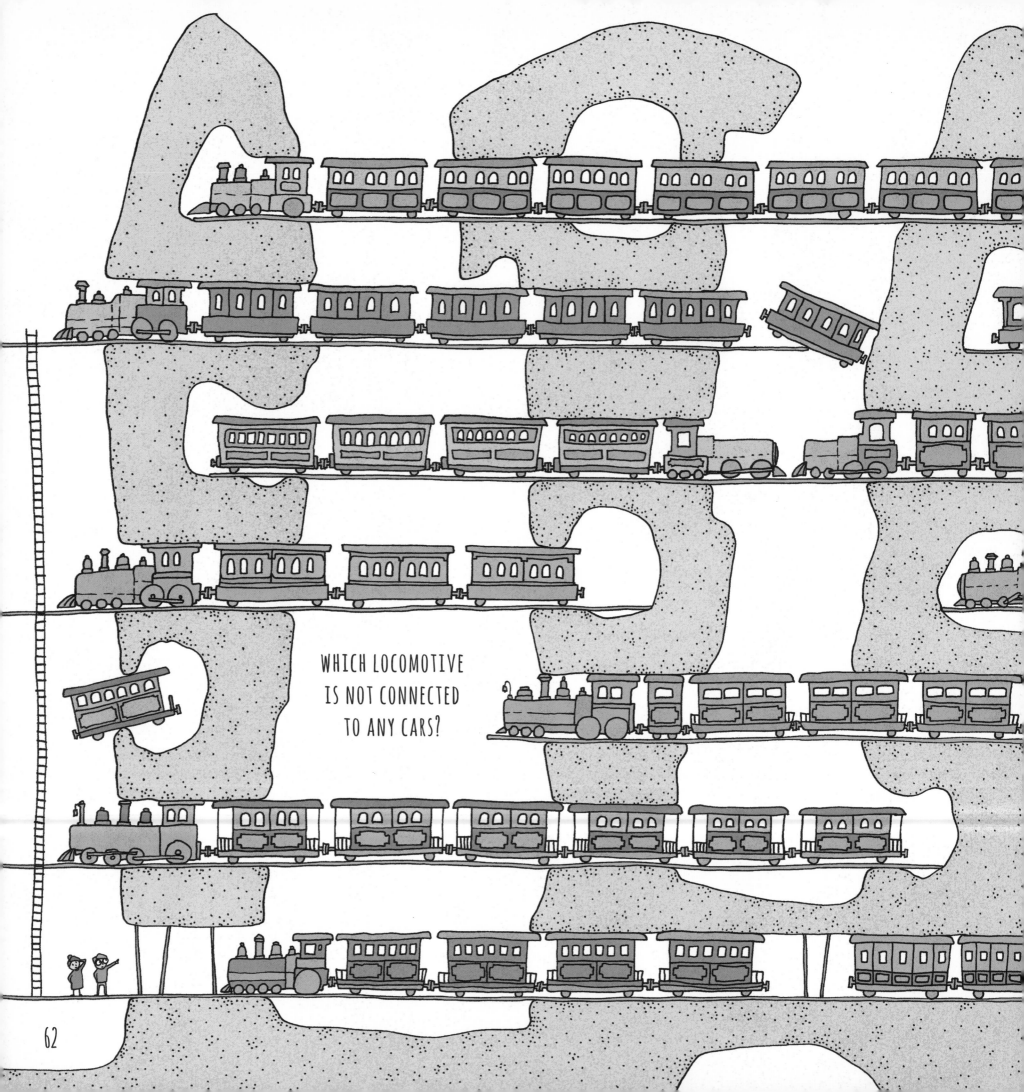

WHICH LOCOMOTIVE
IS NOT CONNECTED
TO ANY CARS?

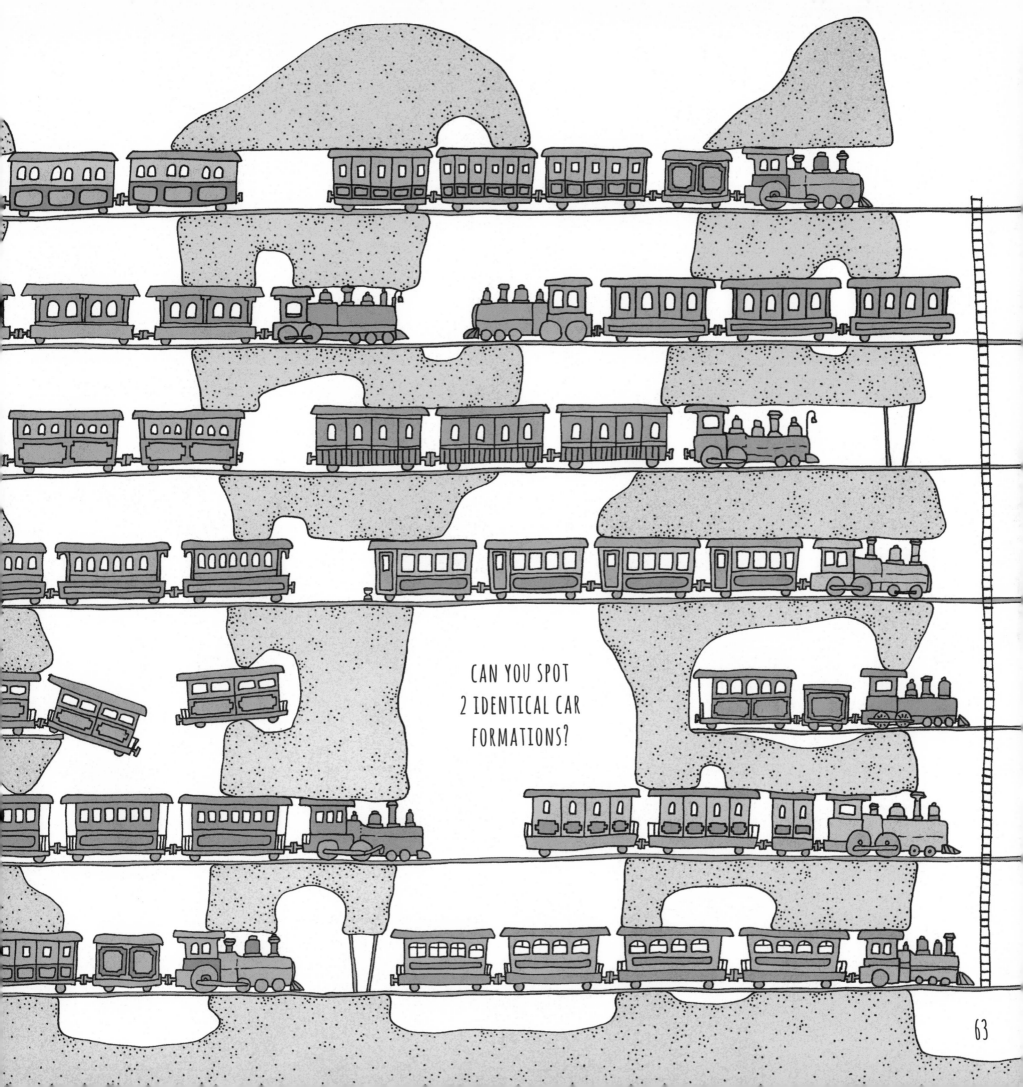

CAN YOU SPOT
2 IDENTICAL CAR
FORMATIONS?

63

LOOK FOR THE HIDDEN KEY THAT WILL START THE LOCOMOTIVE'S ENGINE.

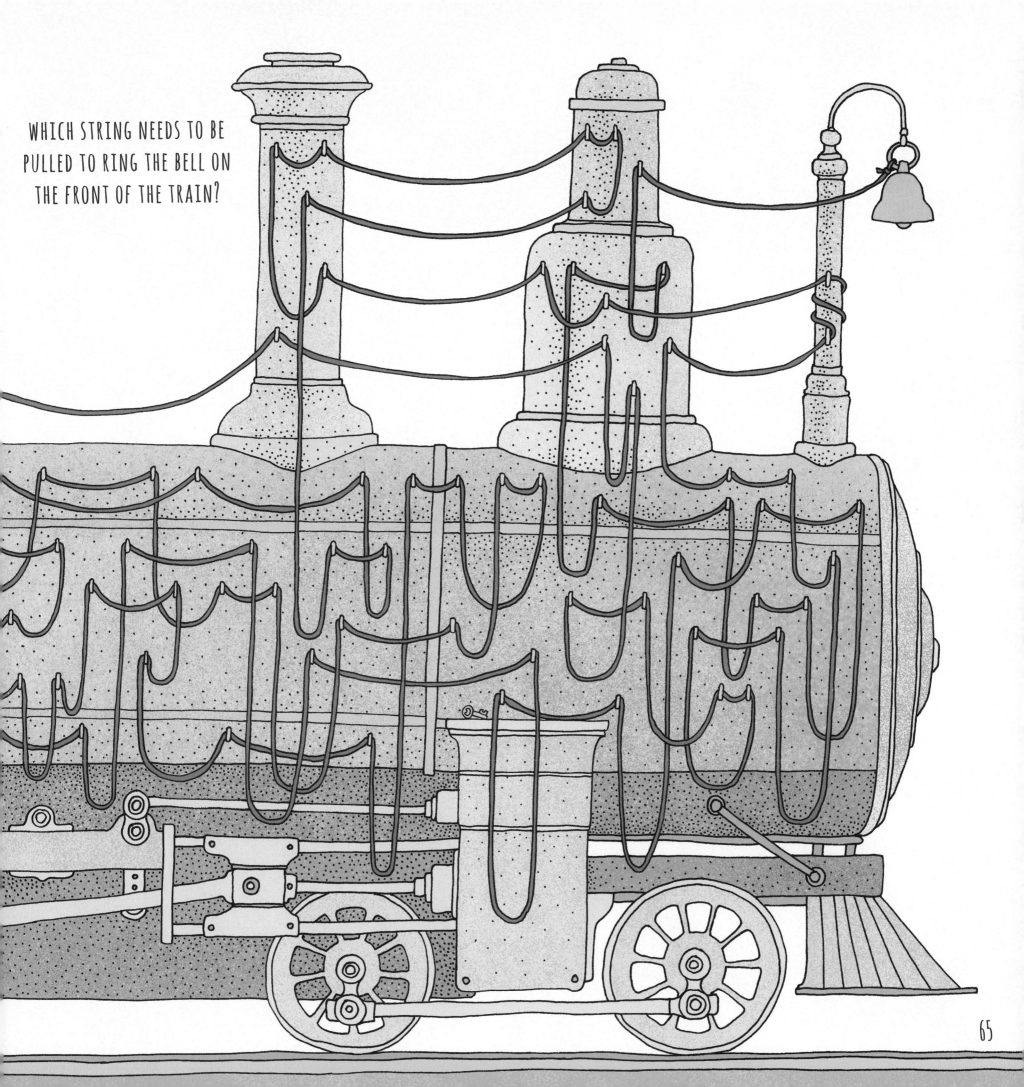

WHICH STRING NEEDS TO BE PULLED TO RING THE BELL ON THE FRONT OF THE TRAIN?

65

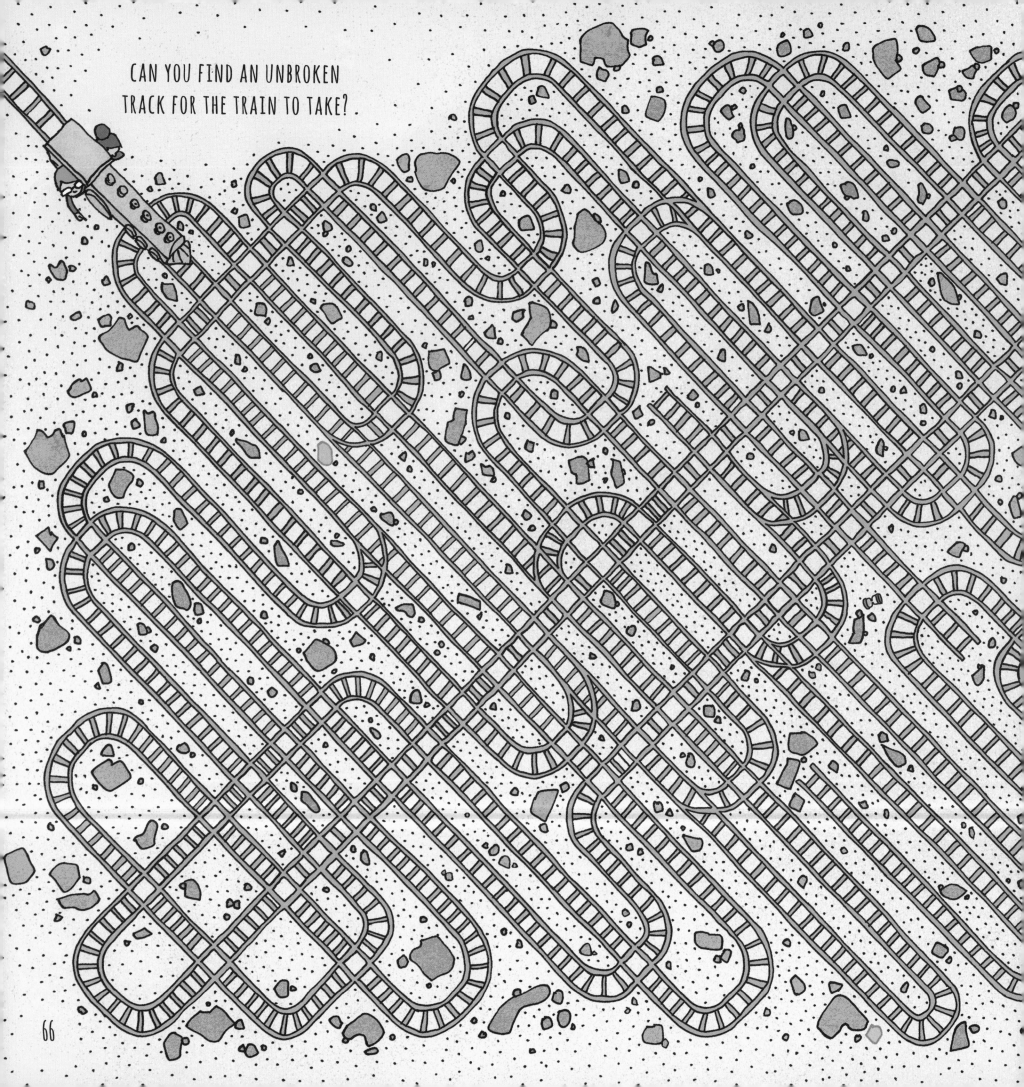

CAN YOU FIND AN UNBROKEN TRACK FOR THE TRAIN TO TAKE?

66

SEE IF YOU CAN SPOT 5
GOLD NUGGETS AMONG THE
DESERT ROCKS.

FIND A SAFE PATH TO
THE ARROW, AVOIDING
ALL THE RATTLESNAKES.

CAN YOU SEE ONE RAM WITH CURLY HORNS AMONG THE BISON?

CAN YOU SPOT THE 3 WAGONS WITH HORIZONTAL STRIPES?

LOOK FOR 3 LOOSE WAGON WHEELS IN THE SCENE.

71

SOME OF THESE
BUILDINGS HAVE
MISSING STAIRCASES.
WHICH ONE HAS
STAIRS ALL THE WAY
TO THE ROOF?

FIND 2 UMBRELLAS HIDDEN ON THE BUILDINGS.

CAN YOU ARRANGE THE STATUE PIECES IN THE RIGHT ORDER, FROM TOP TO BOTTOM?

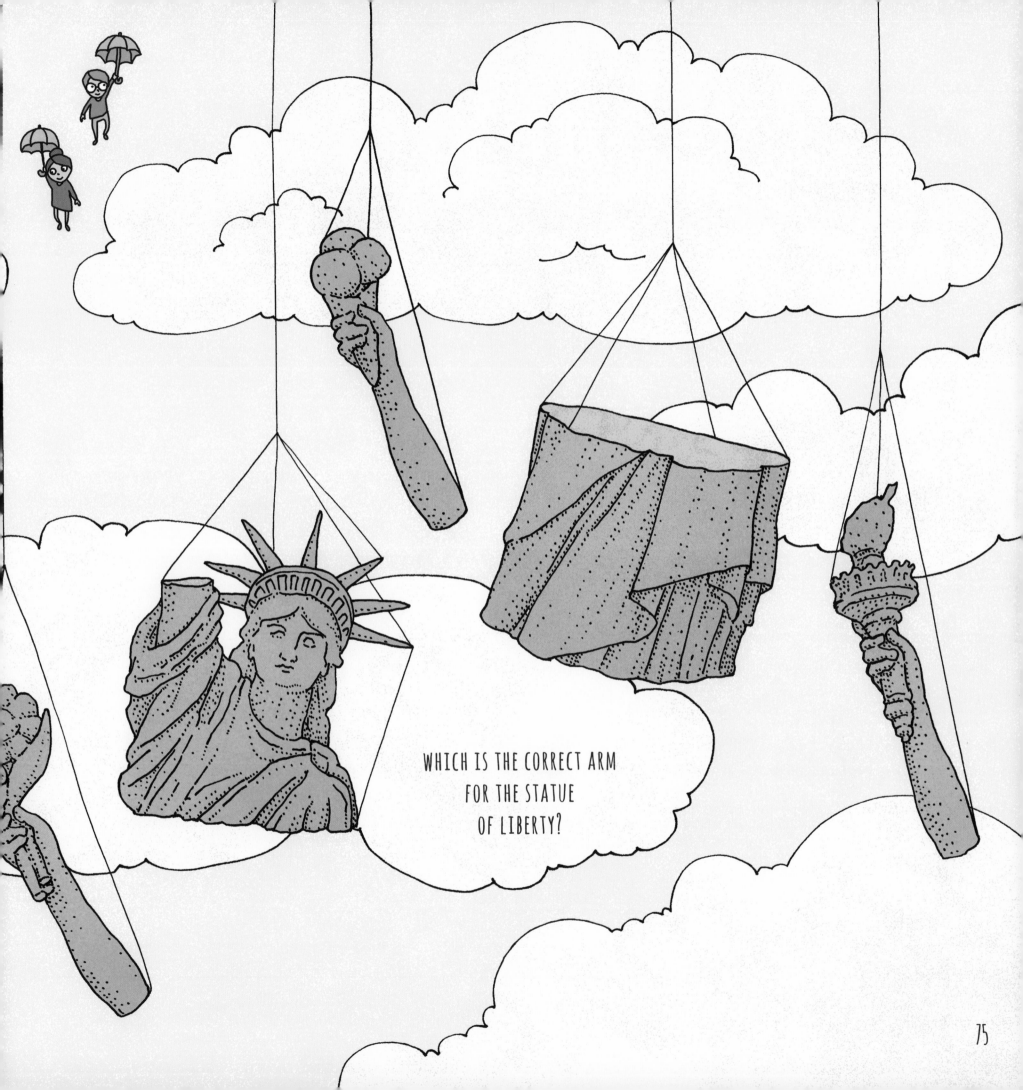

75

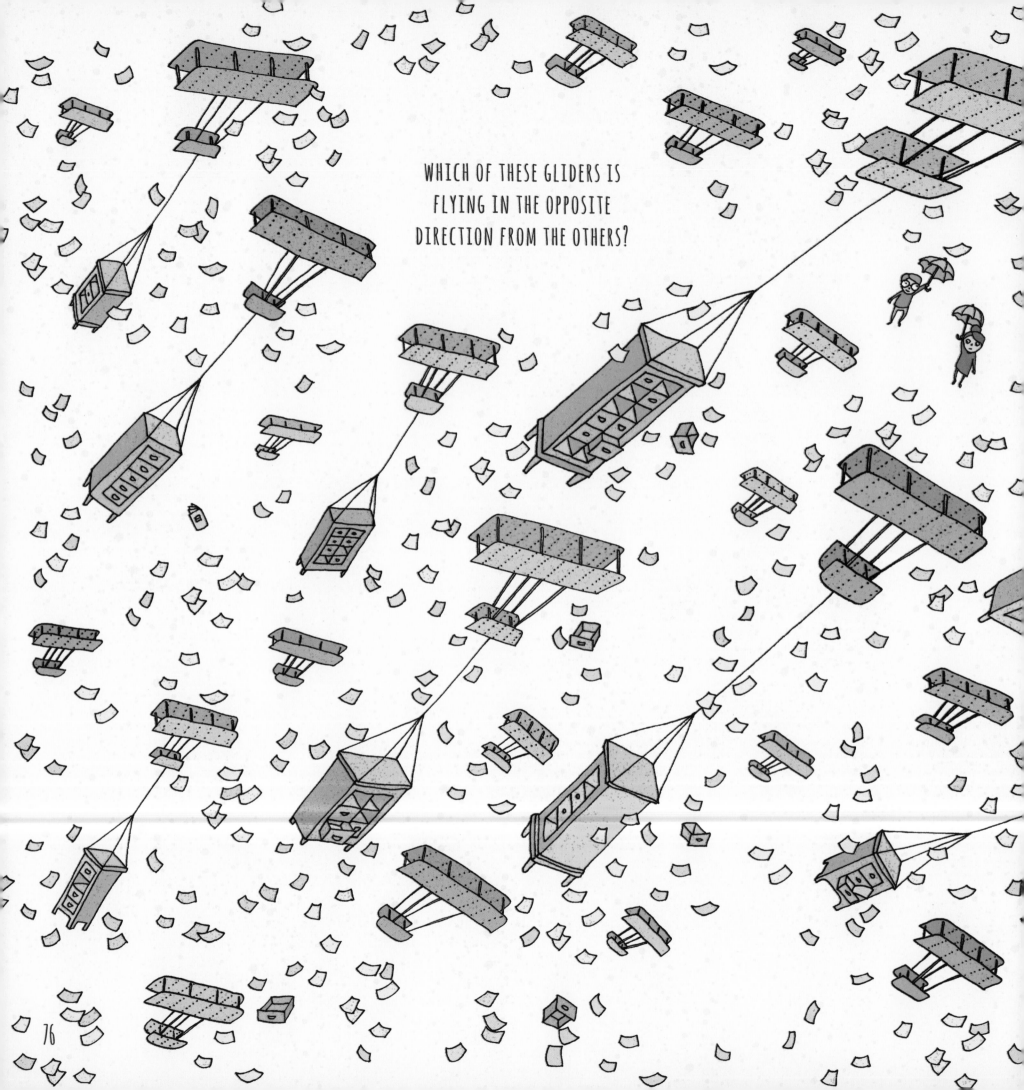

WHICH OF THESE GLIDERS IS FLYING IN THE OPPOSITE DIRECTION FROM THE OTHERS?

CAN YOU SPOT
3 NOTEBOOKS THAT
HAVE FALLEN OUT OF
THE CABINETS?

11

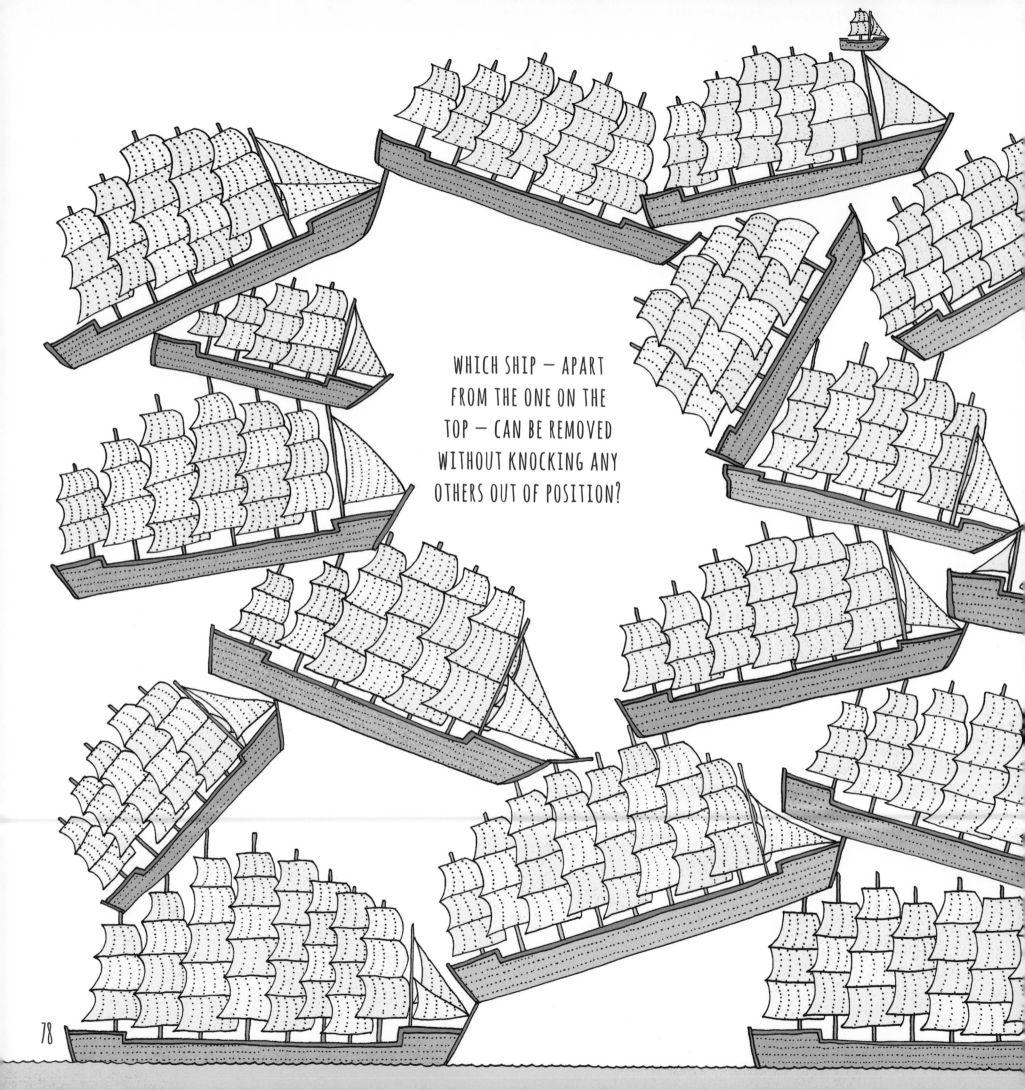

WHICH SHIP — APART FROM THE ONE ON THE TOP — CAN BE REMOVED WITHOUT KNOCKING ANY OTHERS OUT OF POSITION?

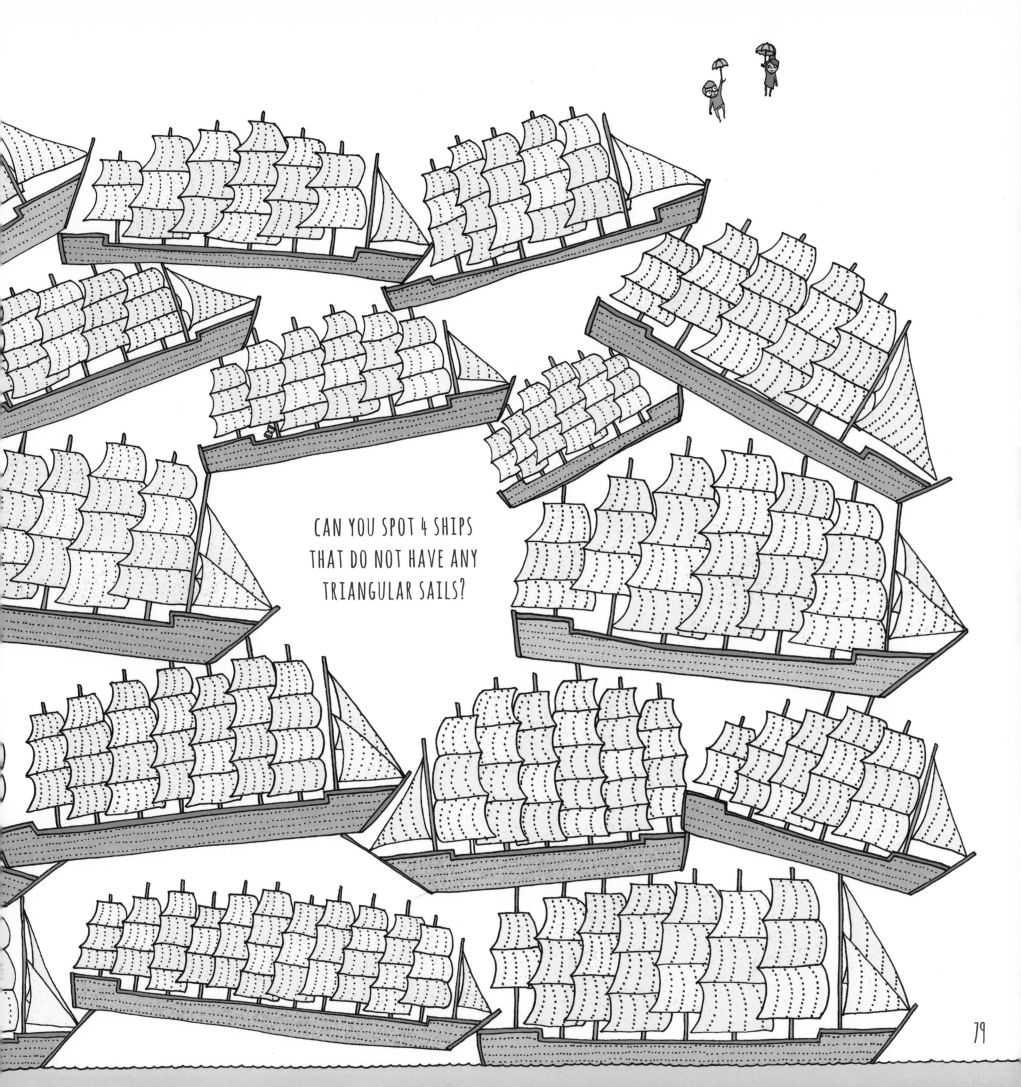

CAN YOU SPOT 4 SHIPS
THAT DO NOT HAVE ANY
TRIANGULAR SAILS?

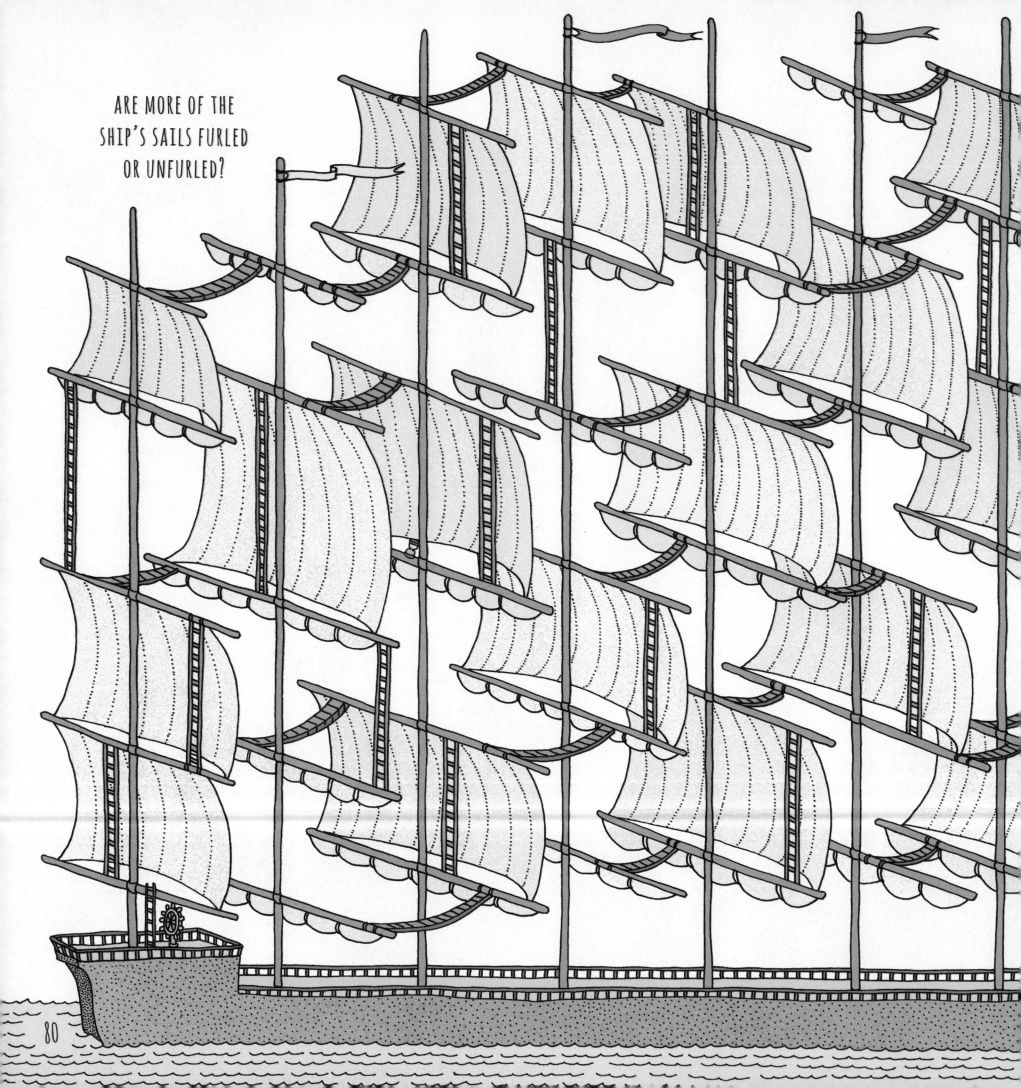

ARE MORE OF THE
SHIP'S SAILS FURLED
OR UNFURLED?

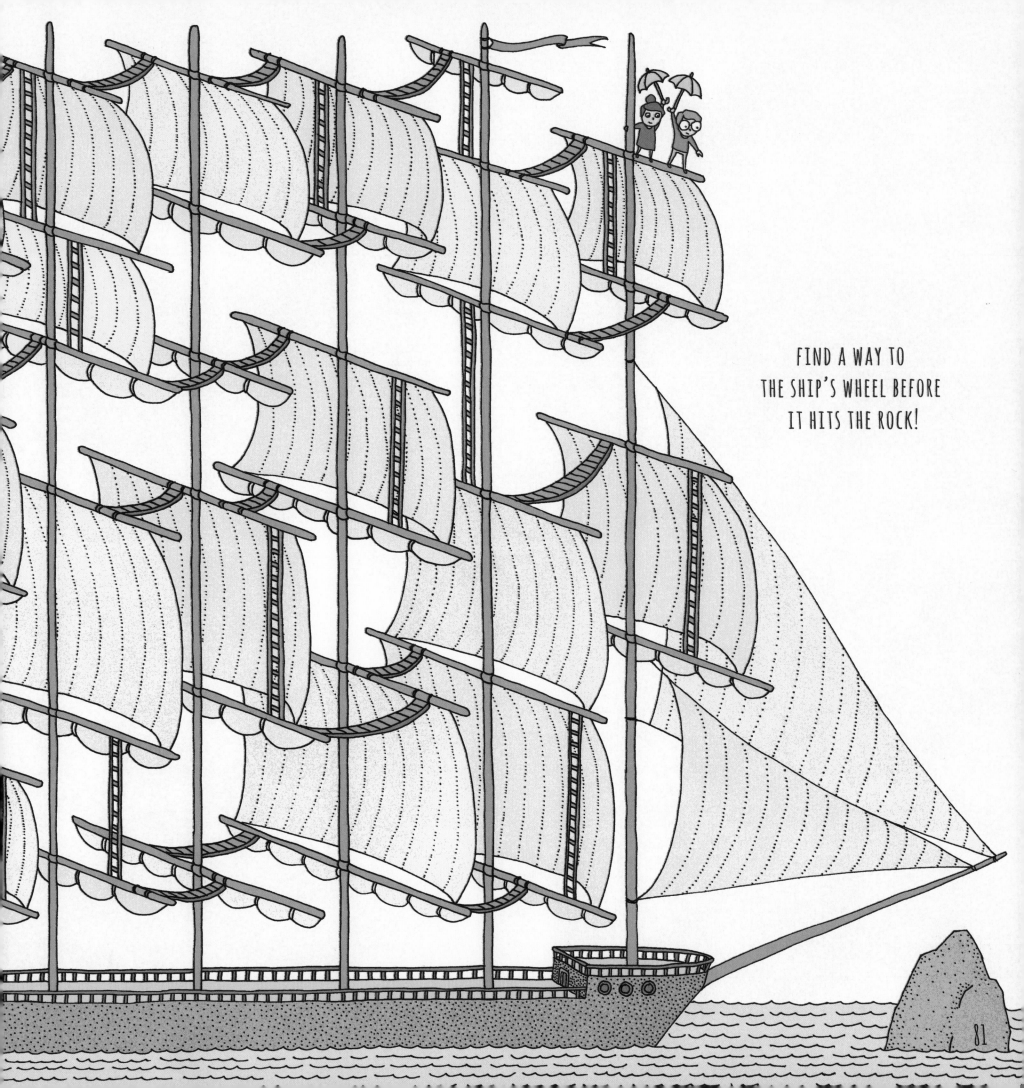

FIND A WAY TO
THE SHIP'S WHEEL BEFORE
IT HITS THE ROCK!

WHICH 3 LIGHTHOUSES
DO NOT HAVE PROPELLERS
ON THEIR ROOFS?

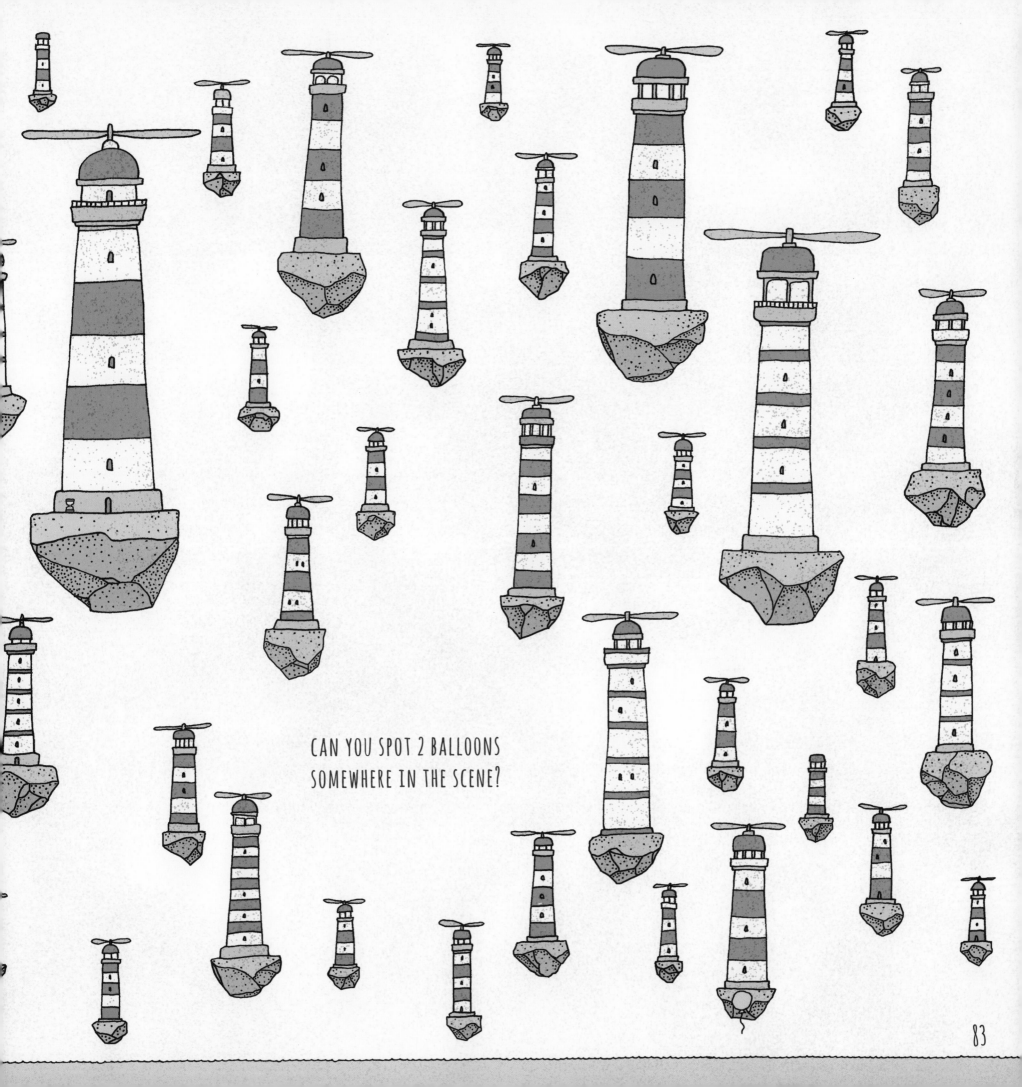

CAN YOU SPOT 2 BALLOONS
SOMEWHERE IN THE SCENE?

THERE ARE 3 DIFFERENCES BETWEEN THE TWO HALVES OF TOWER BRIDGE. WHAT ARE THEY?

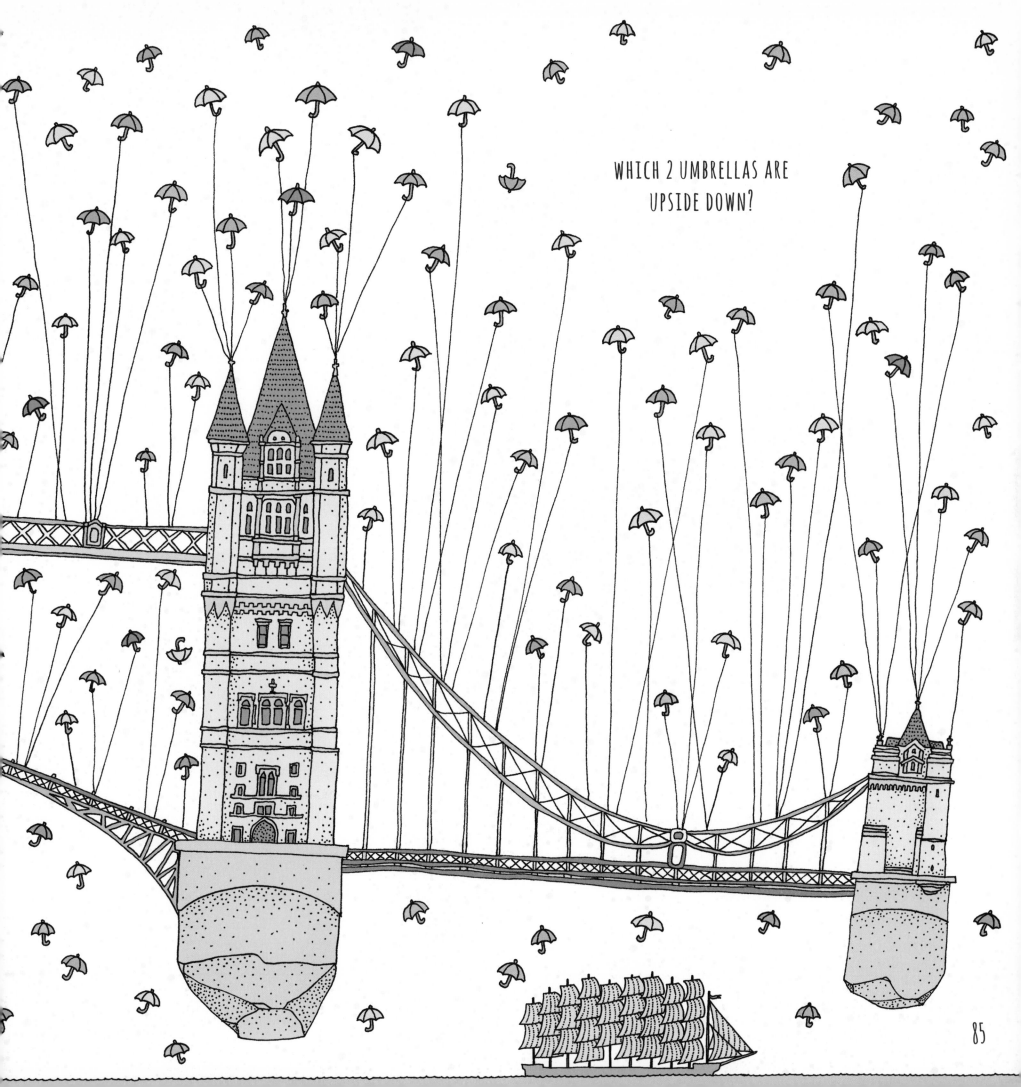

WHICH 2 UMBRELLAS ARE
UPSIDE DOWN?

3 OF THE POCKET WATCHES TELL A DIFFERENT TIME FROM BIG BEN — WHICH ONES?

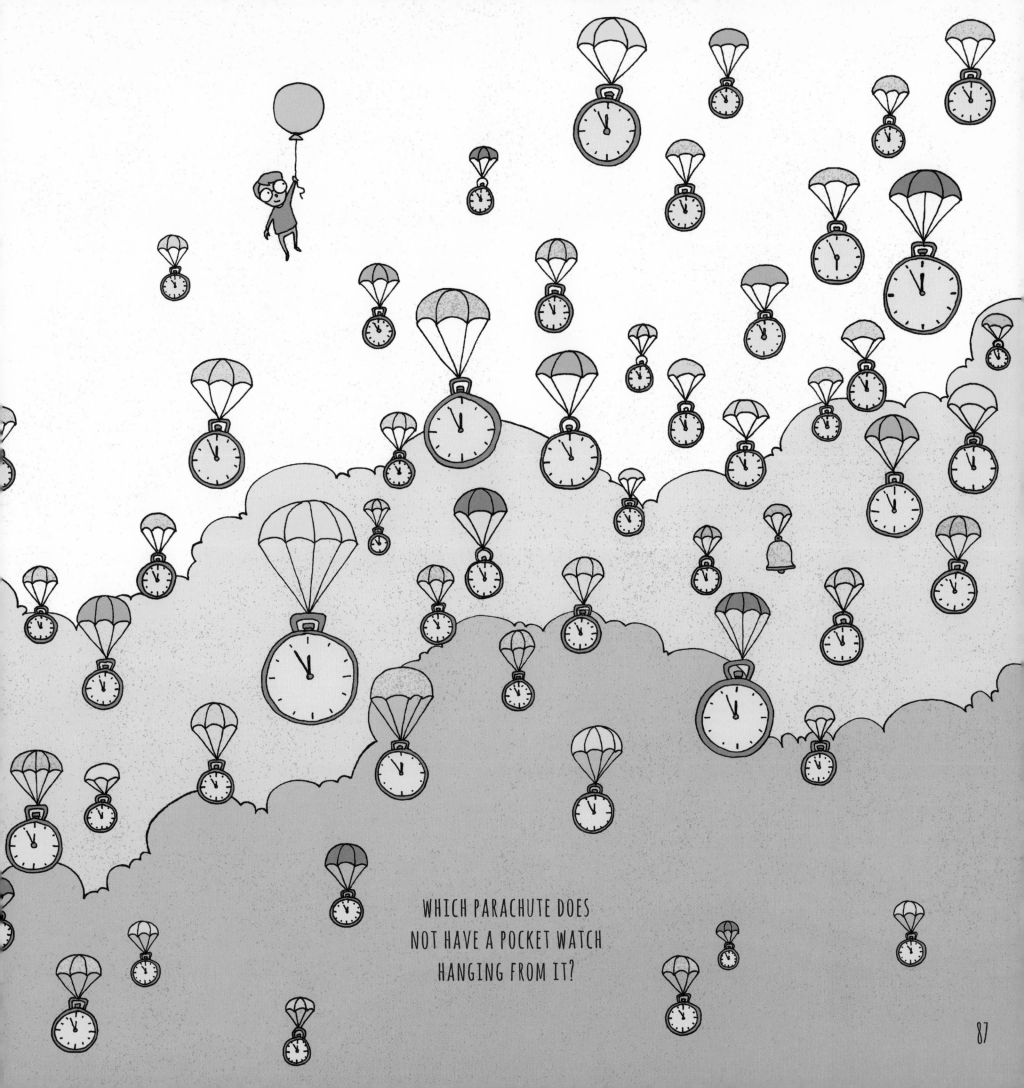

WHICH PARACHUTE DOES
NOT HAVE A POCKET WATCH
HANGING FROM IT?

ABOUT THIS BOOK

THIS BOOK IS INSPIRED BY THE NOVEL *AROUND THE WORLD IN 80 DAYS* BY JULES VERNE.

IN THE YEAR 1872, IN THE HEART OF VICTORIAN LONDON,
PHILEAS FOGG MAKES AN EXTRAORDINARY BET: THAT HE CAN TRAVEL THE CIRCUMFERENCE
OF THE GLOBE IN NO MORE THAN 80 DAYS. THE ENIGMATIC ENGLISHMAN AND
HIS VALET SET OFF ON A BREAKNECK EXPEDITION. TRAVELING BY STEAM TRAIN,
SAILBOAT, AND EVEN ELEPHANT, THEY FACE ADVERSITY AND ADVENTURE AS THEY
TRAVEL THROUGH EUROPE, ASIA, AND AMERICA IN A RACE AGAINST TIME . . .

ANSWERS

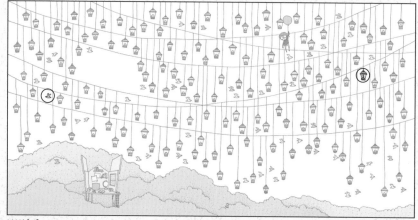

PAGES 8–9

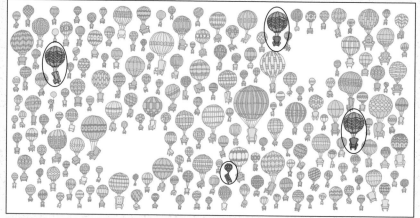

PAGES 10–11

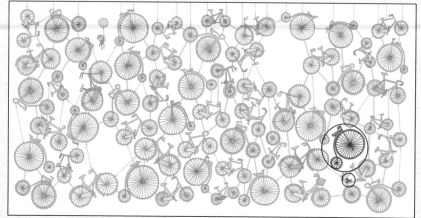

PAGES 12–13

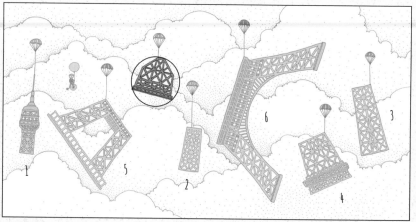

PAGES 14–15

"I WILL BET £20,000 AGAINST ANYONE WHO WISHES THAT I WILL MAKE THE TOUR OF THE WORLD IN EIGHTY DAYS OR LESS; IN NINETEEN HUNDRED AND TWENTY HOURS, OR A HUNDRED AND FIFTEEN THOUSAND TWO HUNDRED MINUTES. DO YOU ACCEPT?"

— PHILEAS FOGG IN *AROUND THE WORLD IN 80 DAYS*

DID YOU SPOT IT?

DID YOU SEE THE HOURGLASS ON EVERY PAGE?
GO BACK AND SEE IF YOU CAN FIND IT.

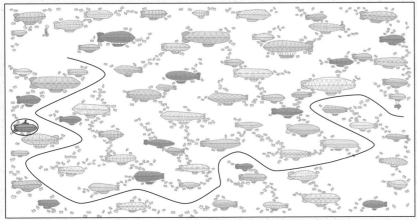

PAGES 16–17

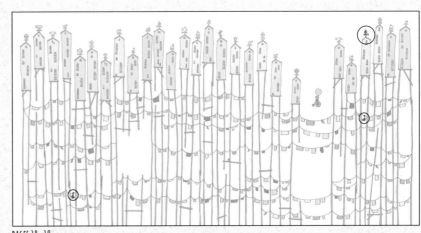

PAGES 18–19

PAGES 20–21

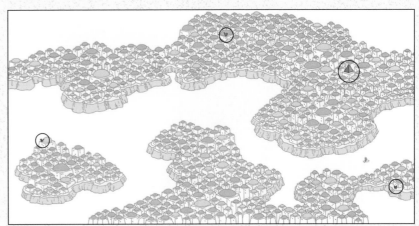

PAGES 22–23

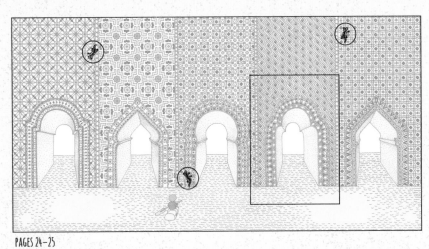

PAGES 24–25

PAGES 26–27

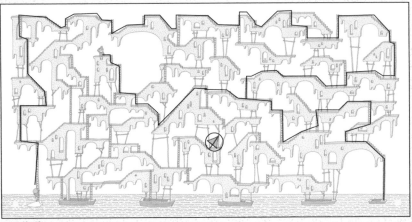

PAGES 28–29

PAGES 30–31

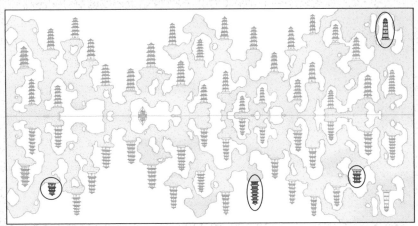

PAGES 32–33

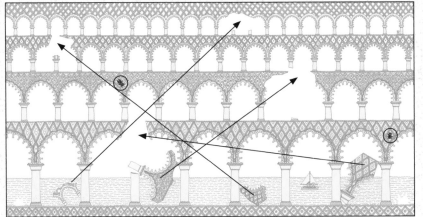

PAGES 34–35

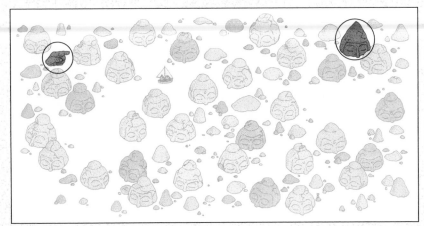

PAGES 36–37

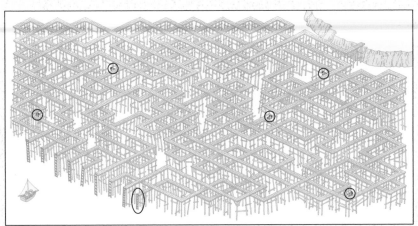

PAGES 38–39

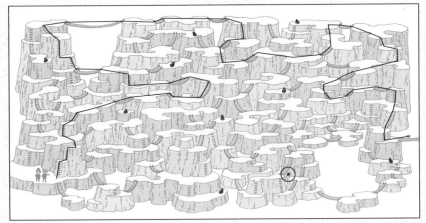

PAGES 40–41

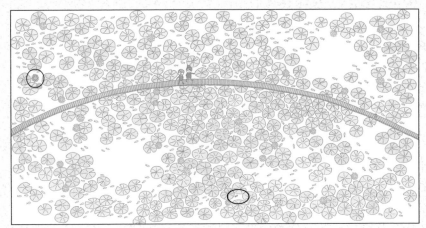

PAGES 42–43

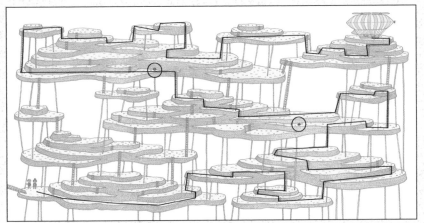

PAGES 44–45

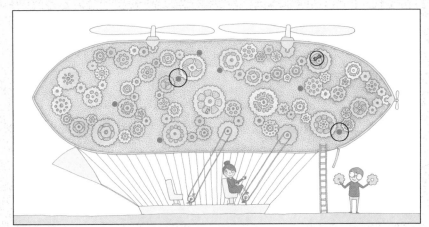

PAGES 46–47

26 KITES 29 KITES

PAGES 48–49

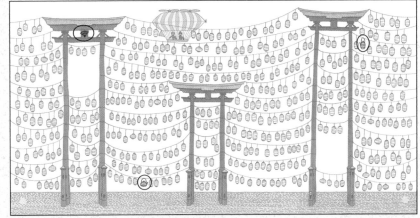

PAGES 50–51

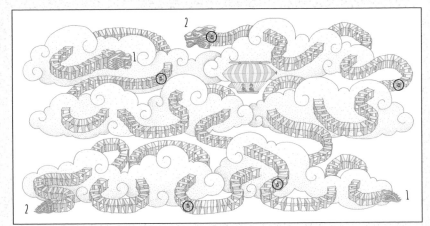

PAGES 52–53

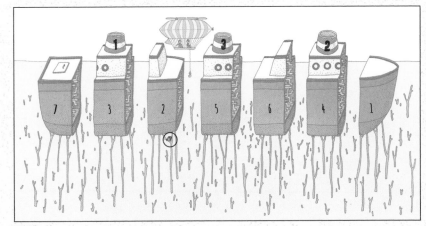

PAGES 54–55

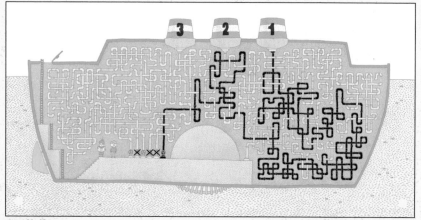

PAGES 56–57

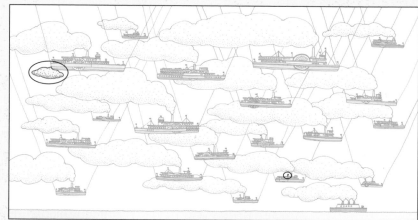

PAGES 58–59

PAGES 60–61

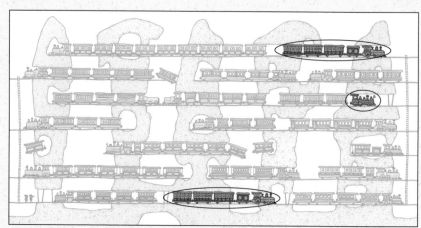

PAGES 62–63

PAGES 64–65

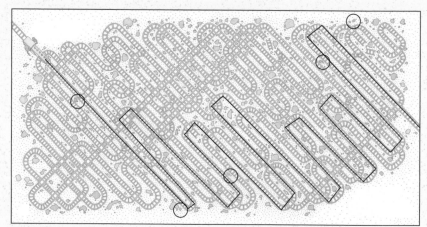

PAGES 66–67

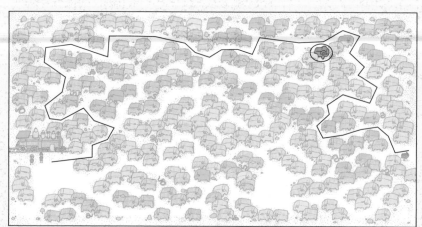

PAGES 68–69

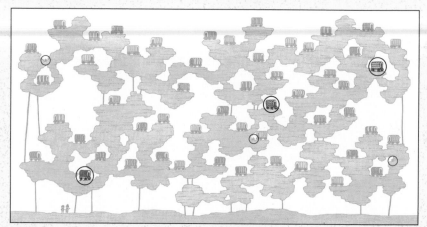

PAGES 70–71